About the Author

Born in Melbourne, Australia, Gavin Catt has always loved science fiction and he feels that science fiction can become science fact. During the day, Gavin works at a major hospital in Melbourne and at night, is reading sci-fi novels, astrophysics books and enjoys sci-fi movies. *The Dimension War* is his fourth book in the Sanctuary series.

The Dimension War

Gavin Catt

The Dimension War

Olympia Publishers
London

www.olympiapublishers.com
OLYMPIA PAPERBACK EDITION

Copyright © Gavin Catt 2023

The right of Gavin Catt to be identified as author of
this work has been asserted in accordance with sections 77 and 78 of
the Copyright, Designs and Patents Act 1988.

All Rights Reserved

No reproduction, copy or transmission of this publication
may be made without written permission.
No paragraph of this publication may be reproduced,
copied or transmitted save with the written permission of the publisher,
or in accordance with the provisions
of the Copyright Act 1956 (as amended).

Any person who commits any unauthorised act in relation to
this publication may be liable to criminal
prosecution and civil claims for damage.

A CIP catalogue record for this title is
available from the British Library.

ISBN: 978-1-80439-404-5

This is a work of fiction.
Names, characters, places and incidents originate from the writer's
imagination. Any resemblance to actual persons, living or dead, is
purely coincidental.

First Published in 2023

Olympia Publishers
Tallis House
2 Tallis Street
London
EC4Y 0AB

Printed in Great Britain

Dedication

Dedicated to Her Majesty Queen Elizabeth II for her tireless and dedicated service of seventy years to the Commonwealth and to countries where she was the head of state.

Acknowledgements

Thanks to the dedicated and professional team at Olympia Publishers for their outstanding efforts and I look forward to working with Olympia on my future projects.

Introduction

It has been six months since Kathryn, Charles, Michelle, my daughter Caroline, Noor's sister Susan, and I returned from Mars, not long after the core of the planet was successfully restarted which was a crucial step of Project Genesis. Over this six-month period, the core of the red planet has stabilised, and now it rotates normally, just as it did three and a half billion years ago. Therefore, Mars now has a stable magnetic field which shields the surface of the planet from solar radiation, and this achievement is a triumph for the White Commonwealth, and the Sanctuary Vega Union was pleased too.

However, on our return to Earth, I received the news that my uncle King George of Proxima Centauri was tragically killed during a state visit to Andromeda. I already knew that my uncle was an expert on the Dimension War, and that he studied it for decades. Plus, I knew that the research that he did would pass onto me on the day that he dies. King George's research covers twenty-four billion years, or to put it another way, from ten billion years before the Dimension War to today. All this research is stored on data chips in my private office.

The Council of Crowns and I decided that I was to devote as much time as possible to sifting through the Aladdin's cave of my uncle's scientific research. I have asked Kathryn and Charles to look after the day-to-day running of the White Commonwealth, so that I would not be distracted, and allow me to process the information. I would still be the head of state of the White

Commonwealth, and the Presiding Monarch of the Council of Crowns. I knew that the Council of Crowns would be able to assist me too.

The Council of Crowns is required to support me as head of state, and I knew that they were just as keen as I was to get started. The Council knew that I was familiar with the methods used by King George to research and store information. I was going to sort the sheep from the goats in my uncle's research and I would not be alone, as Michelle offered to assist me, and so did other members of the royal family when they have spare time.

King George had spent so long on his Dimension War research that both the Sanctuary Vega Union and the Multiverse Council respected his knowledge and experience. There are hundreds of hours of vid and audio recordings as well as terabytes of documents stored on the data chips.

King George's knowledge assisted the Sanctuary Vega Union, confirming facts from early in Sanctuary's history that they were unsure about. He worked closely with the official Sanctuary Archivist who I had met on my mission to meet with Link One of 'The Tower,' and I admit that he helped me fill in many gaps in my own knowledge of the Dimension War.

Even though I was grieving my uncle's loss, I was excited that I was going to learn so much from King George's research, and I was looking forward to learning new things.

The memorial service for King George was conducted two weeks ago, and it was a sad day for everyone, and dignitaries from across the cosmos attended the memorial service. Sanctuary had assisted the Andromeda and the Milky Way galaxies in investigating the cause of King George's death. The result of the investigation was that King George's shuttlecraft was docking with his IGAL starship when a large asteroid collided with both spacecraft. No trace was found of either King George, his shuttlecraft or his IGAL starship.

On the surface of the asteroid, an unusual impact crater fifty kilometres across and five kilometres deep and with a glass-like floor was found, and this indicated that the asteroid hit both spacecraft at high speed. Scientists from the Sanctuary Vega Union concluded that the impact velocity was 35% of the speed of light.

I found it difficult to accept that my uncle was caught completely off guard. I know that my uncle was aware of this asteroid and its retrograde orbit around a neutron star. It was accepted that elevated levels of radiation blinded the proximity alert systems of both spacecraft, and I was certain that my uncle did not suffer.

The collision of the asteroid with the two spacecraft caused the asteroid to leave its orbit and travel out of its solar system, and the asteroid is expected to leave the Andromeda Galaxy in two hundred years and travel in the direction of Stanton's Void. This had me wondering if remnants of the former Dark Empire had something to do with it, and if they did, I had to find out the reason.

Chapter One

The First Session

The night before I was due to start my review of King George's Dimension War research, I slept soundly for most of the night until I woke up lying on my side, facing the bay window and terrace of my apartment. I look at the time: three a.m. Michelle was still asleep, going by the sound of her breathing. I could see a full moon, and there were no clouds in the sky. I lay quietly, not wanting to wake my wife. I hear Michelle stir and yawn softly, and I could feel her moving on the bed.

"Can't you sleep?" Michelle asks in a sleepy voice.

I turn to face Michelle.

"I woke up a few minutes ago, my love," I answer, looking at my beautiful wife. Without saying a word, we move closer to each other. Michelle smiles tiredly as she caresses my side, and I do the same for her. She laughs softly, as she caresses my side again.

"What?" I ask in confusion.

"How do you feel about me having another baby?" Michelle asks.

I think for a moment as Michelle waits expectantly.

"Sounds good to me, my love," I answer, and Michelle's face brightens in the moonlight.

"Let's get some more sleep; we may wake the neighbours," I say, and Michelle replies thoughtfully, "Okay. You are right," and we kiss, and we fall asleep in each other's arms.

Michelle and I wake up at seven fifteen a.m., and we both refresh, changing into casual clothes. Once we are dressed, we walk to the Informal Dining Room for breakfast, and as we walk, Michelle lightly touches my shoulder, and we stop close to the door of the Informal Dining Room.

Michelle asks, "When are you going to start looking at King George's research on the Dimension War?"

"After breakfast. I have a short audience with Admiral M first, and then I will start," I reply, looking at Michelle.

Michelle nods, and then she asks, "Are you doing your research in your Private Office Study?"

"Great guess, my love," I reply, and I give Michelle a kiss on the cheek, making her blush which amused our escort, who was smiling. I nod slightly, and one member of the escort checks the dining room, and returns nodding to me, and Michelle and I enter the Informal Dining Room.

After Michelle and I finish our breakfast, we sit drinking coffee and we chat, as we both had nearly thirty minutes free. As we talked, I noticed Kathryn and Charles arrive in the room. Michelle could tell that I was looking at something, so she turns around and sees them walking over to the autochef and the serving area. After collecting their breakfast, Kathryn sees Michelle and I watching, so she comes over, followed by a distracted Charles. I nod that it is okay to sit down, and Kathryn and Charles sit on the remaining two chairs at our table.

A few minutes later, Kathryn, Charles, Michelle, and I talk casually; while Kathryn and Charles eat, I see Rebecca enter the dining room and as Rebecca passes by our table, I invite her to sit down. After dragging a chair over from a nearby vacant table, Rebecca starts to sit down and Charles shoots her an annoyed look, and he starts to open his mouth. Witnessing the exchange between Charles and Rebecca, and seeing a concerned look on Kathryn's face, I say:

"Prince Charles, I know that there are only four chairs at this table. Rebecca has the right to sit here, and she is sitting here because I said she could. I do not want to have to speak about your rudeness again. I do not know what is going on in your head lately, and I want to remind you that what I said to you at Freedom Hall stands. Sort yourself out," I say with disgust, glaring at Charles.

I could see that Rebecca was upset by Charles, going by the strained look on her face. Gently, I say to Rebecca, "I am sorry, Rebecca. Charles has a nasty habit of not thinking about what he says." I see Michelle and Kathryn nod, clearly agreeing with what I said. Rebecca nods gratefully and smiles at me and she turns to face Charles.

Pointing my finger at Charles, I command, "Apologise to Princess Rebecca, Charles. Right now." Charles looks at Rebecca, and mumbles, "Sorry."

Rebecca, who is still upset, replies, "Thank you, Cousin," and then she looks at me. I could tell by the look on Rebecca's face that she still was not satisfied by Charles's apology, and that she was concerned about Charles's erratic behaviour lately. I nod to Rebecca, indicating that there may be a medical reason for Charles's behaviour. Kathryn looks me in the eye when I face her, and I could tell that Kathryn had had some sort of disagreement with Charles earlier, and I knew that she was worried too.

Changing the subject, I ask Kathryn and Rebecca about their plans for the day. I ignored Charles on purpose, to gauge his reaction. Kathryn tells me that she has two meetings, and then after lunch, she will be playing minigolf with Charles, and then she will be able to have a restful afternoon. Rebecca tells me that she has a week off, and not worrying about being on call for a few weeks. I give Rebecca a thumbs up, and Michelle says that she is spending the day with Caroline.

I kiss Michelle on the cheek, because I knew that Michelle needed the rest, and I say, "You have been working too hard lately, my love." Michelle faces me, and we kiss.

"How about you, Your Majesty?" Charles asks me, in an almost normal tone of voice. Pretending not to notice Charles's attempt to brown-nose me, I reply, "I have my routine audience with Admiral M, and then I will be adjourning to my Private Office Study to start looking at King George's research on the Dimension War. If anyone is free, please feel free to join me."

Rebecca says that she will join me, and Michelle says that she will join me later. Charles has a blank look on his face, so I knew not to expect him as he appeared to be sulking. Kathryn says, "After the minigolf, I plan to join you."

After my audience with Admiral M, Rebecca joins me in my Private Office Study, and we sit looking at the briefcase-sized container, full of data chips, which is on the coffee table in front of us. Rebecca looks at me and says, "Thank you for what you said to Charles in the Informal Dining Room, Cousin William."

"No problem, Rebecca," I reply, seeing Rebecca smile.

I say thoughtfully, "As we work through these data chips, I will need to take notes."

"Can I help?" Rebecca asks expectantly.

I consider Rebecca's offer, and I reply, "Only if you want to. I take it that you know the method I use?" I ask, knowing the answer.

"You were a great teacher, Cousin Will," Rebecca replies nodding.

"Let's get started," I say with a smile, as I reach forward, and I take out the first data chip that I can see.

Data chips are rectangular in shape, five centimetres long by one centimetre wide, and one centimetre deep. I look at the title 'Trade,' and I moan slightly, and Rebecca looks at me with concern. "Are you all right?" she asks.

"Fit as a Mallee bull," I reply, showing Rebecca the title.

"Could be interesting?" Rebecca says, with a smile. I pick up my screenpad, which was linked to the viewscreen, and I place the data chip in the reader port.

I enter the special code that King George had given me, knowing that it is correct. A menu appears on the viewscreen. Scrolling through the menu options, I ask, "Any suggestions?"

"How about 'General Overview'? I saw that at the top of the menu," Rebecca says helpfully.

"Select 'General Overview'," I say to the viewscreen, and two new options appear, 'Multiverse Trade' and 'Internal Universal Trade'.

"The agony of choice," I say looking at Rebecca.

Rebecca smiles, saying, "'Multiverse Trade' is a good start."

"Thanks, Becky," I say, smiling at my cousin.

"Select 'Multiverse Trade'," I say.

A dialog box appears on-screen, containing a vid.

"Play Vid," I say.

On-screen, the Sanctuary Vega Union logo appears, and then a Cilex appears in a Picture-in-Picture screen, introducing the subject.

"Trade between the remaining universes, and within individual universes, is more important today, than it was billions of years ago. Goods, Services, as well as Tourism, is important to many economies, from the Multiverse, to within universes, galaxies, planets and habitats," drones the monotone voice of the Cilex. The Cilex pauses momentarily, and then says, "Prior to the Dimension War, trade between universes was not as common as today, due to frequent border disputes."

"Sounds just like the Earth during the late twentieth century, and through the twenty-first century," Rebecca says.

"Business School 101," I reply with a shrug.

The Cilex arrives at its key point, "However, some disputes became serious," the Cilex says, as it appeared to look straight at me.

"Uncle George must have had a reason for including this vid on the data chip, Cousin William. My question is why?" Rebecca asks thoughtfully.

I think carefully, and then I reply, "You're quite right, Becky. I think that Uncle George had found out why the Golden Sceptre was created." Rebecca looks at me closely, knowing that I was uncomfortable by the sound of what I had just said.

I point a finger at myself.

Rebecca asks with concern, "Why include this particular vid on this data chip?"

"Do you remember how he liked using codes, or games that resembled code breaking?" I ask, and Rebecca nods slowly. "The Golden Sceptre is the key, and he must have worked out that I will eventually 'merge' with the Sceptre," I say with uncertainty, and then I say, "the note taking is twofold. Firstly, it helps me process the information and secondly, it confirms to me which code King George used."

"What do you mean?" Rebecca asks in a puzzled voice.

Suddenly, the reason dawns on me. "The Golden Sceptre itself ended the Dimension War, and it unified warring universes and galaxies. It is the ultimate peacemaker," I say with increasing dread. The vid finishes playing, and the menu re-appears.

Rebecca and I sit quietly, looking at each other. "I have asked myself why the Golden Sceptre chose me, and Caroline as my heir. When I was told that the 'merger' will take place, I started to understand that I either resembled its creator or, that it has always existed, and the Golden Sceptre knew when I would appear. It is possible that I am the Golden Sceptre in human form," I say with a shrug, stunned by what I had just said.

Rebecca replies, "Strangely, that makes sense to me, and we already knew that your destiny was predetermined by the Golden Sceptre. Obviously, King George worked this out, and do you think your own father knew?" Rebecca asks.

"King Douglas knew. So did the Multiverse Council and the Sanctuary Vega Union. It freaks me out, to be perfectly honest," I explain.

"So that is why you feel uncomfortable, cousin," Rebecca says sympathetically.

"I am who I am, William Gavin IV, King of the White Commonwealth and Presiding Monarch of the Council of Crowns. I know that I am not a God, otherwise I would be a good minigolfer," I say with a grin.

Rebecca laughs at my joke, and she pats me on the shoulder with her hand.

"You have always been incredibly good to me, and you sorted out Drago too. I will always be grateful to you, Cousin Will. If I can help you sort this out, I will, and I care about you as if you were my own brother. Are you going to tell the others?" Rebecca asks kindly.

Nodding slowly, I say, "Kathryn, Michelle and you are my rock. I will not discuss this in detail with anyone, for obvious reasons. However, I am certain that Michelle and Kathryn know about this already. Bugger it, it will make enjoyable conversation at lunch. So, I will bring it up.”

“Do you mean, the *lunch*?” Rebecca asks, trying to keep a straight face.

I can barely keep a straight face myself, which makes Rebecca laugh, and I reply, “The issue at hand, not lunch,” I say with a grin on my face.

“We can come back to this after lunch,” I say, pointing at the viewscreen. The time on the grandfather clock in my study, which previously belonged to my father, indicated eleven thirty a.m.

Chapter Two

Lunch

Rebecca and I walk slowly towards the Informal Dining Room, chatting casually.

"I have been thinking about what you said in your study," Rebecca says, as we arrive at the entrance to the Informal Dining Room. A member of the Palace Guard waits patiently for us to finish talking. "About the merging?" I ask, suspecting what Rebecca's question will be.

"That's right. When does the merger occur?" Rebecca asks.

I look into Rebecca's eyes, and I reply:

"When I die."

Rebecca looks at me with concern.

"I am not crazy about the idea, but I have discussed this with A1 Shentar, and Queen Madeira of Vega. They both have said the same thing: the Sisss that I know personally was around during the Dimension War and has offered to help me to understand the process of the merging, and about the Golden Sceptre itself. Without it, the Sanctuary Vega Union would not exist, and neither would we. Cheerful subject to talk about, isn't it?" I ask.

Rebecca considers my point, and she replies, "Like I said, I will help you to understand it, if I can. Please ask me, and we can work it out together."

"Thanks, Rebecca," I say gratefully, and I nod to the waiting guard who checks the room, and she says, "You can go in now,

Your Highness."

Rebecca and I enter the Informal Dining Room, and as we do, we can see Kathryn, Charles and Michelle sitting at a nearby table talking. Kathryn sees me and she nods, smiling as Rebecca and I arrive at the table. I gesture for the others to stay seated, as Rebecca and I sit down. I sit on Michelle's right and Rebecca sits at the end of the table. My sister and Charles are opposite Michelle and me. Our lunch arrives not long after, and as one, we start to eat.

I notice Kathryn staring at me, cocking her head slightly in Charles's direction. Understanding Kathryn's silent message, I nod slightly. The message was clear: Kathryn and Charles have been arguing, and I wondered why.

After lunch, as a group, we all go and sit in the lounge area, and I talked about what I learnt from King George's research. As we talk, the body language between Kathryn and Charles appeared to be relaxed for now.

"This first data chip, on 'Trade,' is just an overview so far. However, the common thread in this material is the Golden Sceptre, and hints at its true purpose. How it connects to me, is yet to be determined. I will say this, Caroline is connected as well," I say, and Michelle looks at me in surprise. Michelle and I had discussed this point once we became aware that the merger between the Golden Sceptre and I would take place, but I had left Caroline out of it. Looking at Michelle, I could see that she was considering what I had just said.

"You can see why I left this out, Michelle. I did not want Caroline to worry about something that she cannot control, and I didn't want to confuse her when I was still not quite sure myself," I explain, as the others watched.

Michelle replies, "Have you considered asking the Sisss, or

Link One about this?"

I answer. "I have a planned meeting with the Sisss in the Delegate's Council Chambers at Sanctuary, on Multiverse business next week, so I will ask then," I say, as I note what I just said on my screenpad to remind me. Michelle nods as she places a hand on my shoulder to reassure me that she accepted my explanation.

Kathryn glances at Michelle, and then she asks me, "I am free for the rest of the day. Why don't you and Michelle join Charles and I, in a thirty-six-hole game of minigolf, and then we can join you in your study after that?"

I look at Michelle, who nods, and I reply, "Great idea. I could do with a break," and Rebecca smiles, knowing that I needed some relaxation.

I was smiling after the minigolf game because I played very well, much to Kathryn's surprise. A couple of times, I glanced at Michelle as we walked to my study.

"You need to relax, when you are about to play your shot," Michelle says.

"Yes, coach," I say, causing Michelle to frown.

"Are you still worried about the merger?" Michelle says sympathetically.

"That is right, my love. I am thinking about how this will work for Caroline," I say. Michelle nods as we arrive at the door to my Private Office Suite. We enter the office suite and then we enter my study and sit down. The others had not arrived yet, so we continued our conversation.

"Caroline will work it out. I have been guiding her and answering her questions. Our daughter will be fine, Will. Please do not worry, you have enough to worry about," Michelle says as she puts her arm around my shoulders, and kisses my cheek.

"Thanks, beautiful girl," I reply, as the others enter my study, and sit down.

"Play the 'General Overview' vid," I say to the viewscreen, after placing the data chip that Rebecca and I looked at earlier into the data chip reader.

Rebecca and I watch the reactions of Kathryn, Charles, and Michelle. Michelle and Kathryn did not seem to be surprised, but Charles had a blank look on his face. This did not surprise me, and I could tell that Rebecca was thinking the same way as me.

When the vid finishes, Michelle says, "Now I can see why you are concerned, Will. I know that you have accepted your destiny, and that you have no choice in the merger with the Golden Sceptre. You are more concerned about placing a burden like this on Caroline's shoulders. Am I correct?" Michelle asks me.

"That's right," I say, as I reach forward to pick up my coffee cup.

Kathryn says, "I know that the rest of the family wants to support you, Will. You are realistic, knowing that you cannot shirk your responsibilities, and at the same time, you care about this being a burden for everyone. Let us help you. I spoke to Ann, Elizabeth and Marina on the way to your study, and they want to help you too," Kathryn says, seeing that I was getting uncomfortable with the discussion.

To my complete surprise, Charles says, "I know that things have not being going too well lately, and I have annoyed you, Your Highness. Whenever the Golden Sceptre was created, or even if it has always existed, I will say this, the Golden Sceptre's purpose is to merge with you, no matter when it was created, and you will fulfill its own destiny." Charles stares at his shoes, and everyone else stares at me, waiting for my reaction. I hold my hand up to indicate "please, give me a moment" and I think about what Charles said. I had been thinking that way, but I was too focused on my own issues.

Looking at Charles, I say, "Prince Charles, you have hit the nail on the head. Thank you. If you have any ideas that will help me, feel free to suggest them to me.

"Am I truly human then?" I ask, and I was surprised that no one appeared to be shocked by what I said.

"Peace in the Multiverse, and in this universe as well, is only possible because of the Golden Sceptre, and you are the key," Kathryn says, looking at me. I nod slowly. Rebecca looks at me closely, and she nods in understanding.

Chapter Three

Dinner

In the Informal Dining Room, Michelle, Caroline, and I enjoy dinner together. On a nearby table, Kathryn, Charles, Rebecca, and Marina are having dinner as well. I watch Kathryn and Charles closely, and everything appears to be normal.

"Why do you keep looking at Charles and Kathryn?" Michelle asks, as she continues to eat.

"Have you noticed anything unusual going on between them lately?" I ask, looking at Michelle. Going by the look on Michelle's face, I could tell that she was thinking carefully.

"Now that you mention it, I have. They have been arguing lately about trivial things, which is so unlike them," Michelle answers, returning my stare.

"That's what I thought, and I have concluded that Charles may be sick," I explain.

Michelle nods, "That is what I have been thinking," Michelle says.

"His personality seems to have changed since he was a part of the negotiation team, in the first high-level discussions with the Zlay High Councillor."

Michelle leans forward, and asks me quietly, "Do you think that he has contracted CovZlay?" Michelle asks. I nod slowly. "Can we do anything for him?" Michelle asks with concern.

I answer quietly, "Pray that it isn't that. What I will do is that

I will speak to Kathryn privately, and I will need to contact Sanctuary Medical for assistance, and I will advise both the Sanctuary Vega Union and the Multiverse Council. CovZlay is not contagious, and it rarely affects humans, but when it does, the patients do not usually die."

Michelle was stunned, but she knew that I was right. "Does the Council of Crowns know yet?" Michelle asks, looking in Charles's direction. "They do, except Kathryn and Charles," I say with some regret, looking at Kathryn's table. Kathryn and the others had just finished their evening meal, and that is when Kathryn notices me looking at her. She stands up and walks over to our table. I give Michelle a quick look, knowing that she will understand what I want her to do.

I invite Kathryn to sit down, and I explain to her my concerns. At first, Kathryn shoots me an angry look, and I could see that she was thinking carefully about what I said. Kathryn nods slowly, understanding my concerns. "It explains a lot, Will. I am sorry that I doubted you at first," Kathryn concedes. I look into my sister's eyes, knowing that she was as worried as I am.

"What can we do?" Kathryn asks.

"Watch him closely, without being obvious and that is what Rebecca and Marina have been doing. I should have told you earlier, but with CovZlay, you cannot take any chances," I say, uncomfortable that I had to deceive my sister until I was certain.

Kathryn looks into my eyes, knowing that I had to do something that I did not want to do, and that there was no alternative. She says to me sadly, "Okay, Will. I know that you care, and I know that you had to do something that made you feel uncomfortable. You have done the right thing. Did you want me to say anything to Charles?" Kathryn asks me.

"Not yet. I have contacted Susan for advice," I reply.

Charles, Rebecca, and Marina come over to our table, as a servbot clears the table. Suzi, Caroline's babysitter arrives to prepare Caroline for bed. Once Suzi and Caroline leave the dining room, the others drag spare chairs over to our table, I indicate that is okay to sit down, and we start chatting casually.

"My plan of attack with King George's research is in two parts. Firstly, I will learn what I can, and I will cross reference the facts with my own notes, as I work through every data chip in the storage container. All three hundred data chips, to be exact," I say, pausing to have a sip of coffee.

Continuing, I add, "I will sort out what needs to be passed on to the Council and what is suitable for public release. Secondly, I will be searching for information relevant to the Golden Sceptre, and why I was chosen," I say, looking at the others. I saw sympathetic looks on every face, knowing that they now understood my concerns.

We continued to chat for several minutes, when my personal comcall unit chimes. I pull it out of my polo shirt pocket, and I answer, "What is it?" I ask, and the others fall silent.

"I am sorry to disturb you, King William. The Sanctuary Protocol Office has just been in touch with us. The Sisss Sanctuary Delegate is currently en route to the Milky Way. They have said that as you were due to meet at Sanctuary soon, and they are on their way out to the 'Wanderer', they thought that you would be okay if the meeting occurred sooner and save you a trip to Sanctuary. The Sisss will be arriving tomorrow and will be meeting with you at nine a.m.," Assistant Bacon explains.

"Thanks, Aisha, that's fine. Can you pass on my thanks to the Sisss and tell them that I look forward to meeting with them? Aisha, feel free to take the evening off, and I will see you tomorrow at nine a.m.," I reply.

"Thank you, sir. Enjoy your evening," my assistant says.

"No problem," I answer, signing off, and I see expectant looks on the faces watching me.

I explain the comcall in detail. "Isn't it the first time that a Sisss has been to Earth?" Charles asks, sounding as normal as I could expect, considering the suspected CovZlay.

"That's right, Charles," I reply.

I tell the others that the transfer apparatus that the Sisss like to travel in looks like a propane gas tank for a barbecue. I explain that they are more comfortable travelling in this fashion, and that they will be releasing themselves from the tank for the meeting. I explain the human-like sense of humour that the Sisss have, and I ask if anyone would like to meet the Sisss. Everyone is interested, including Charles who looked bored. I select Michelle, Rebecca, and Marina, and I ask Kathryn and Charles to take notes. Charles's expression changes again, and I notice, Kathryn and Charles agree. Kathryn glances at me, knowing exactly what I want her to do. Kathryn nods in understanding.

As soon as I have concluded the informal meeting, I knew that I had a free evening too. Michelle and I stand, and we walk over to the Lounge Area for drinks with Rebecca, Kathryn, and Charles.

"I know that you think that my humour is a little strange; wait until the formal part of the meeting tomorrow is over, and we talk casually with the Sisss. They have fourteen billion years of jokes to tell," I say with a smile.

Chapter Four

The Sisss

After a pleasant night's sleep with Michelle, Michelle and I are joined by Rebecca and Marina for breakfast. Kathryn and Charles join us later for coffee, and I remind them of the protocols of formal meetings with a Sisss. Thankfully, it is the same as formal meetings between humans.

We all return briefly to our apartments, to change for the meeting. At nine a.m., we arrive as a group in the audience room, and we finalise our arrangements on a raised dais.

I sit on a standard executive office chair, which serves as my "throne" in this situation. Michelle, Kathryn, Charles, Rebecca, and Marina sit on normal office chairs, and we all face the door that the Sisss will use.

At nine thirty a.m. exactly, a hand trolley is wheeled into the room, and the transfer device is unloaded by a couple of Royal Guards. After a guard takes the trolley out of the room, the Sisss releases themselves from the gas bottle. A human shape is formed from the cloud that fills a part of the room. The Sisss greets us formally, and I introduce the members of the family that are in the room. Once the formal greetings are complete, the meeting starts.

The Sisss explains in detail what will happen to me during the merger with the Golden Sceptre. After answering a couple of questions from Michelle, the Sisss assures me that they understood that I was nervous, and they offered to guide me through the process again, to ensure that I was comfortable.

Finally, the Sisss offers to assist me with King George's research, as they had assisted my uncle during his research project for the Sanctuary Vega Union and the Multiverse Council. I assure the Sisss that I will make use of their kind offer soon.

Once the official part of the meeting was over, the Sisss chatted casually with us and shared some very amusing anecdotes until a Royal Guard returned with the hand trolley and the transfer apparatus. After making their formal farewell, the Sisss returns to the transfer apparatus, and leaves the audience room.

Kathryn, Charles, Michelle, Rebecca, Marina, and I go into my Private Office Study, and we sit down after getting coffee from the autochef in the room.

After we all sit down, I ask, "What do you think?"

Kathryn looks at me closely, watching my face. "Now I can see why that you have been so anxious lately. To have your destiny predetermined by someone outside our time, but intimately connected to our time, is the cause of your distress."

Then Marina says, looking at Kathryn and I, "Sounds logical, strange as it seems." The others nod with concern, giving me sympathetic looks.

Michelle asks, "Will, do you think that your father, King Douglas, knew about this?"

"Michelle has a point," I think and then I exchange a glance with my sister. Kathryn nods, and I understand that she was thinking about this too, and I reply to Michelle, "It is possible, considering what was concealed from my sister and I. There is nothing that proves this, in King George's research, but I get the strange feeling that my father knew," I say as I glance at my sister.

Kathryn nods in agreement with me.

After drinking some water, Kathryn says thoughtfully, "I have been thinking about what you have just said, Will. I am certain that our father knew this, and that it was hidden to protect you. It is like the situation with me, three years ago. The Council of Crowns would not know about this, as this is too sensitive to discuss." Kathryn has a look of horror on her face, realising what she said to me. It made perfect sense to me.

"For now, we need to do the same. If the circumstances change, then we can discuss this further. Are we agreed?" I ask.

"Yes, Your Highness," everyone replies.

Chapter Five

The Second Session

After lunch, Michelle and I relax in the Lounge Area of the Informal Dining Room, chatting casually and drinking coffee. Several minutes later, we are joined by Kathryn, Charles, Rebecca, and Marina, and I indicate that it is okay to sit down.

In all seriousness, I look at each face, and I ask, "If anyone has any questions about what we discussed earlier, please come directly to me." Michelle glances at the others, and then she turns to face me, "No problem, Will. We all understand," she says, and the others give me a sympathetic look.

As there was nothing else needing to be discussed, everyone leaves to deal with their scheduled tasks, but I was glad that Michelle and Rebecca were free to join me.

"Now is as suitable time as any, to return to King George's research," I say to my wife and cousin. The three of us leave the lounge area and return to my study.

"Would you like me to take notes?" Rebecca asks me as we sit down.

Nodding, I reply, "Yes, please, Becky, and I will take audio notes as well," I add as I take out my personal audio recorder from my polo shirt pocket and place it on the coffee table. I reach for the 'Multiverse Political Structure' data chip which is in the container, and I grin at Michelle and Rebecca. "Last chance," I say, with a grin.

After placing the data chip in the reader, I look at the viewscreen. To my dismay, the contents menu has over twenty-one points, and I look at Michelle and Rebecca.

"Get ready to be bored then," I say, trying not to laugh. Michelle and Rebecca exchange glances and Rebecca says with a smile,

"Try 'Contents Overview', cousin."

I select the suggested item, and the Sanctuary Vega Union logo appears on-screen, and the vid itself starts to play.

This time, a Zel female appears on-screen and says, "I am Zir-Ah of Zel. My position at Sanctuary is as head of the Multiverse Archives on Shentar, and I specialise in political science. With me is King George of the White Kingdom. He is the former presiding monarch of the Council of Crowns, and he is currently the King of Proxima Centauri in the Milky Way Galaxy."

I look closely at Michelle and Rebecca, and I could see that they had not expected this, and neither did I, but I was not totally surprised. When King George appears on-screen, I could see that he looked much younger. Rebecca stares at King George, and says, "How long ago do you think that this vid was made?" For a moment, I think very carefully, and I recalled something that my father had said.

"About fifteen years ago," I say slowly. I touch the pause icon, and I activate the facial recognition system on my screenpad. Moments later, my screenpad beeps five times.

Looking at the screen, I read the answer. "It was twenty years ago," I say. I look carefully at Michelle and Rebecca, and Rebecca says, "King Douglas had a disagreement with my father about Drago, but I do not remember much, as I was only about eleven years old at the time."

Michelle gives me a strange look. I could see that Rebecca was becoming upset. I say kindly, knowing that Rebecca knew anyway, "Please try not to worry about this too much. My father admitted to my mother, the reason," I say, as I stand up, and I sit down on the arm of the sofa, next to Rebecca, and I place a hand on her shoulder, knowing how much she suffered at the hands of her brother.

"We will say no more about it, and you also know that I cannot discuss this in detail," I say, but my tone of voice indicating that I wanted to say more.

Rebecca looks at me closely, and I could see some tears in her eyes.

"Are you okay?" I ask with kindness.

"Yes, cousin. I know that you are doing your duty, and that you are not able to discuss anything in detail." I give Rebecca's shoulders a reassuring squeeze, and then I go back and sit next to Michelle. "Thank you, cousin," Rebecca says, and she gives me a thumbs up.

Michelle says, "It's a comparable situation between you and Kathryn."

I look at Michelle knowing that she is right, and I say, "That's right, my love."

I resume playback of the vid, and the image of King George's face unfreezes, and he resumes speaking. He tells us that before the Dimension War, universes were grouped into four main classes of Multiverse society.

Members of the Political Class ran the day-to-day affairs of life in every universe, and they appointed members of other classes into governmental positions. The purpose of the Military Class was to defend their appointed societies from attack by other beings, and they appointed the Civilian Police Forces to enforce the laws passed by the Political Class. Members of the Privileged Class owned businesses and employed members of the Civilian Class.

Beings in every class of the pre-Dimension War Multiverse resided together in ordered societies, and usually in peace. What the Privileged Class did not know was that they were reviled and distrusted by the members of other classes. The main question was for how much longer?

At this point, the vid finishes playing, and the next title appears on the viewscreen, 'The Military Class', and a dialog box appears asking if I want to continue.

I look at the others, and I say, "As riveting as the overview was, I am taking a break," and I look at my wife and cousin. Both nod in the affirmative, and the three of us go to the Informal Dining Room for some refreshments.

On arrival in the Informal Dining Room, Michelle and I sit down while Rebecca gets some coffee from a barista. Rebecca hands me my coffee first, and then she sits down after giving Michelle her coffee. "Thanks, Beck, it was very kind of you to offer," I say as I have a sip.

"No problem, cousin," Rebecca says with a smile. I take another sip of coffee, waiting for someone to say something about seeing King George. Two minutes later, Michelle asks, "Why King George?"

I look at Michelle, watched by an interested Rebecca. "His expertise in the area. The Multiverse Council and the Sanctuary Vega Union recognised his knowledge, gained over decades. My own studies under King George were no walk in the park," I explain.

"My father had hinted to me that protecting the true identities of Kathryn, you and I, was vitally important," I say.

Michelle and Rebecca exchange a look and Michelle says carefully, "Now I understand what you mean. Sanctuary knew how important you are, in relation to your destiny, Will. That is why the three of us required protection." I nod sadly, and I could see that Michelle and Rebecca were concerned, going by the looks on their faces.

I face Rebecca, and I say, "Becky, I understand that you were also protected in this way. Your father, Prince Fredrick was the son of King James, and brother of my own father. Things were hidden from you as well, and if I understood things sooner, I would have told you," I explain, watching Rebecca's face.

She didn't seem terribly surprised, and I look into my cousin's eyes, and Rebecca replies, "I was told some of this by my father, many years ago, but not everything. Cousin William, you have nothing to apologise for." Rebecca smiles at me, knowing that I felt uncomfortable.

Michelle asks logically, "Do we need to change the objective, with King George's research?"

I glance at Rebecca, who nods encouragingly, and I reply, "No. Some of the things we learn from the research will make us uncomfortable, so we need to continue on the current course of action."

"Why?" Michelle asks with confusion.

"Because there is no Plan B," I answer.

I started to tense up visibly, and Michelle and Rebecca both understood why I was becoming nervous again. Their faces showed concern for me, and Michelle says in a soothing voice, "Just relax. We did not mean to upset you."

Rebecca looks closely at me, and she says, "You were doing your duty, and I know that you take things seriously. The burdens that you must carry as our king, are difficult to imagine for the rest of us. I do have one question for you."

"Which is?" I ask.

"Could you refuse to merge with the Golden Sceptre?" Rebecca asks.

Looking at Michelle for support, I reply, "That, Becky, is the sixty-four-thousand-dollar question. I never asked for this, and I am sure that the being outside of our time would have considered that. If I could, I would have rejected it, but the organiser would have considered the possibility. That was a particularly good question, Rebecca," I say, smiling at Rebecca, and Michelle watches in fascination, knowing how close I am to my cousin.

"Uncle George knew about the true purpose of the Golden Sceptre, long before anyone else did in the White Kingdom. My own father, King Douglas, knew as well because he collaborated with King George on the research. My father never told me about it, and King George's cryptic clues when he was teaching me became obvious as I studied Cryptology in the Galactic Navy. That is just one reason my sense of duty is so strong, and not because I was heir to my father's throne. The Multiverse Council, the Sanctuary Vega Union and senior members of the Council of Crowns knew everything. Therefore, things were hidden from us for our protection," I explain, not believing what I had just said.

Michelle and Rebecca exchange glances again as I watch. Michelle smiles at me and says sympathetically, "We will help you as much as we can; please, do not worry. You wear your heart on your sleeve, my love. No one doubts your sense of duty and commitment to the White Commonwealth, neither of us doubt you, and the Council does not either. It is almost like you have to be two separate people at the same time."

I stare at Michelle, and I look at Rebecca saying, "You are right. Thanks for being the logical one, Michelle."

I look at Rebecca, adding, "Becky, you are logical too. Sometimes I just bore myself," I say, laughing and nearly knocking over my nearly empty coffee cup.

We finish our coffee in silence, and Rebecca asks, "Do you think that time travel was used, to protect this timeline?"

Michelle and I look at each other, and I say to Rebecca, "Michelle, Kathryn and I have discussed this recently, and I can say that the Sanctuary Vega Union and the Multiverse Council have always been our protectors, and a high price was paid because the former Dark King Rasputin suspected some of this, but he decided to keep this from Mara once he realised what a loose cannon she is."

Neither Michelle nor Rebecca knew this, I realised, going by the looks on their faces.

I say quietly, and Michelle and Rebecca leaned towards me, "I can't say this too loud. The 'Shadow' was playing the Dark Emperor and King like a harp. As 'Enigma', I created so much doubt in the Dark Empire that they thought it was something else entirely," I say with a satisfied smile.

"They lost sight of many things because the 'Shadow' was responsible for creating the Dark Empire's fear of Intergalactic Technologies," I say enigmatically.

Both Michelle and Rebecca knew that when I went off on a tangent like this, I was hinting that there are far more secret parts to this, and as King, I could not say anything else on the subject. They also knew that I did not like the secrecy, and that I wanted to say more but I could not.

"How do you know this?" Michelle asks, and Rebecca nods.

"I found out more than I wanted to when I was last at Vega. Al Shentar was there too, and he explained that the Kiir set out on the mission to Earth to present the Golden Sceptre to Pharaoh

Khasekhemwy in Ancient Egypt. The mission came from Vega itself, and I can tell you that the Kiir are from Vega. However, they existed in several universes at the same time," I explain carefully.

"That explains a great deal, Will," Michelle says.

The three of us sit in silence until I say, "It is now three p.m., and I have decided not to go back to the research today. I can say that I have my answer about the merger, based on what we have learnt so far, and from our discussion. Merger or no merger, it is time for minigolf."

Rebecca looks at me, saying, "Great idea, cousin," and I see Michelle nodding in agreement.

Chapter Six

The Third Session

For the next forty-eight hours, I purposefully avoid going back to reviewing King George's research in my study. Instead, I concentrated on relaxing by playing minigolf with Michelle and Caroline, because my uncle's research disturbed me deeply, and deep down, I knew that I could not avoid it either. It was a classic Catch-22 situation, and I wanted to learn more. For some reason, I felt that my predetermined destiny was dangerous, and I knew that I had to work this out for myself. The biggest question for me to consider is how I reconcile my destiny with my role as king and as a human being.

When I woke early on Saturday morning, I decide that after breakfast I would resume my own research. No major engagements are scheduled, so I knew that a few members of the family may join me in my quest to find out more. My next major engagement is not for a few days, so time is not an issue. At eight thirty a.m., Michelle, Caroline and I enjoy a leisurely breakfast in the Informal Dining Room, and we are joined by Kathryn, Charles, Rebecca, and Marina.

Ann and Elizabeth had just finished their night shift at the White Palace Medical Service, and they sat drinking coffee at a nearby table. Both looked exhausted, and I had not seen them for several days. I excuse myself, and I stand up and go over to Ann and Elizabeth and I invite them to join us, but Ann and Elizabeth politely declined my invitation.

I was about to turn around and go back to my own table when Ann asks, "How is the research going?" I drag a spare chair over and I sit down, and I bring Ann and Elizabeth up to date on my progress so far. They both knew about my destiny, like the other members of the Royal family and the Council of Crowns, and I could see that they are concerned for me going by the looks on their faces. After assuring them that I was fine, I promised that I would seek their assistance when I needed it. Ann and Elizabeth smiled at me, and I stand up and I return to my own table. I look at Ann and Elizabeth and I see them nod their thanks.

After looking at Charles, Kathryn says to me, "We can join you today."

"Thanks, Kathryn," I reply, glancing at Charles.

In quick succession, Michelle, Rebecca, and Marina, say to me, "I can."

Funnily enough, Caroline says to me, "Me too!" I look at the others who grin like Cheshire cats, and I answer Caroline, "Not today, Caroline. Because you will be helping me, in the future." The others glance at me in surprise, understanding what I was *not* saying: What happens to me, will happen to you. Caroline stares at me with intensity, and I had my answer, Caroline knew everything about the merger and my destiny.

"We may as well go to my study now, so take the opportunity to refresh, and join me in my study at ten thirty a.m.," I say, and everyone concurs by nodding.

At ten-thirty a.m., everyone was in my study, and I insert the data chip into the reader, and then I touch the Play icon on the screenpad. The first part of the vid described the Military Class in the Gtza universe, which create weapons of unimaginable power. I exchange a look with Kathryn and Michelle as this was a reminder of our mission to destroy the mysterious Kiir freighter, which was hijacked by the Dark Empire. The Gtza Military Class created the doom weapons to destroy as many solar systems as possible and rule their universe with fear.

A member of the Gtza union appears on-screen and confirms that the Kiir in their universe confiscated the weapons for themselves, even though the Kiir had developed their own.

The vid finishes and the menu appears on the viewscreen, confirming that the next vid is titled 'Civilian Class'. Glancing at a nearby clock, I say, "We may as well break for lunch, and we will reconvene after lunch."

After lunch, Charles and Kathryn were not able to join me in my study, so Michelle, Rebecca, Marina, and I return together. I start the playback of the final vid on the data chip, and we get to see media reports from the time, which showed tensions rising quickly, which highlighted the plight of the Civilian Class in the border disputes, which was in the 'Civilian Class's' vid. It was no surprise that crime was also on the rise, taking advantage of the border disputes, and crime gangs became more powerful.

Peace was desired by all in the Multiverse, and crime gangs decided to inflame tensions between universes by taking sides in internal conflicts, which created greater tensions and masked their own activities.

It was the Larip, the creator of 'The Tower' that tried to intercede in the border disputes and exposed the criminal gangs for what they were. The clouds of war were gathering on the horizon. Unofficial diplomacy was working and some elements of society, wanted to destroy universal harmony. Jointly, the Multiverse Council and the Sanctuary Vega Union appealed for calm and asked the squabbling parties to see sense.

It was around this time 'The Shadow' started to become

active, and other criminal gangs started to become concerned. For the first time in Multiverse history, criminal gangs started to fight each other. Outright war breaks out between the Sti, Xyro and Ky universes. The Multiverse Council and the Sanctuary Vega Union were powerless to stop the warring parties because of Multiverse law. The Multiverse Council and the Sanctuary Vega Union could only respond if they were being attacked directly.

It was at this point the Kiir were prompted discreetly by Vega to step in and announce that they were going to create a new and peaceful universe, by destroying the Gtza universe and the other warring universes at the same time.

"Pause playback," I say, and everyone looks at me with a look of relief on their faces. I walk over to the small bar in my study, and I put some ice into a glass, and I add a measure of Midori Melon Liqueur. After pouring orange juice into the glass, I stir the drink and I face the others, "You may as well take a break," I say, holding the drink in my hand. One by one, the others come over and get a drink after I move out of the way to make some room at the bar. Sitting down in my usual spot, I take a sip as the others return to where they were sitting.

Once everyone had settled, I say despondently, "I know where this vid is taking us, and I know what is left. This vid was shown to me at Vega, and it shows the true purpose of the Golden Sceptre. You can watch the rest of the vid if you like," and I covered my face with my hands, and I felt drained emotionally. I could tell that Michelle, Rebecca and Marina were looking at me with concern. At this point, Kathryn and Charles arrived and they grasped the situation quickly.

"Now I can see why you were questioning when you will merge with the Golden Sceptre, and, of course, why," Michelle says, touching my shoulder and Marina changes seats and sits down next to me, and she puts her arm around my shoulder saying nothing. "Thanks, guys," I say at last.

"You're welcome, Your Highness," Marina says.

"Could you all excuse me? I need to depart immediately for Brioche, alone," I say as I stand up. After leaving my study, I go straight to the White Palace Hangar and I board the 'Raptor' and depart the Earth.

Chapter Seven

Answers

On the flight to Brioche, I send a courtesy voice message to Queen Noor, letting her know that I will be in the Andromeda Galaxy, and that I may be visiting Freedom Hall on the way home to the Milky Way Galaxy. I also send an apologetic message to Michelle, Kathryn, Charles, Rebecca, and Marina.

"Sorry, I had to leave suddenly, and I was very rude to you all. There is no justification for what I did; however, if you watch the rest of that vid we were watching, you will understand why I must do this alone. I will see you soon, and you all mean a great deal to me," I said in my audio message.

A few minutes after I sent the audio message, the 'Raptor' announces, "King William. I have received an audio message from Queen Kathryn."

"Thanks, 'Raptor'. Can you please play the message?" I ask, as I check the programming of the arrival instructions for Brioche on the control pads in front of me.

The next thing I hear is Kathryn's voice. "Will. That is okay. I have spoken to the others, and they are okay with your message. We saw the rest of the vid, and we understand. Please do not worry."

"End of message," the 'Raptor' says.

"Thank you," I reply, and I sigh with relief as I enter the Andromeda Galaxy.

One hour later, I land on Brioche near 'The Tower', and I discuss my concerns with Link One for about one hour. 'The Tower' listens to my concerns, and I was assured that everything will be all right. Link One told me that the Sanctuary Vega Union and the Multiverse Council were aware of my concerns, and they knew that I would be worried. Link One connects directly with the Multiverse Council, and even brings the mysterious entity that is outside our time into the discussion. I said nothing as this being talked to me, and it told me to rest assured that the merger is nothing to be concerned about.

"Are you God?" I ask it.

"I am not God. However, when you merge with the Golden Sceptre, beings will think that you are God. I am of the Larip. We are guardians of the entire cosmos for you, Golden Sceptre," the Larip said. "In time, you will understand, King William and your daughter, Caroline, will also understand," the Larip adds mysteriously.

The Larip signs off its connection, and Link One says, "Sorry, King William. I was not allowed to tell you, but the Larip had told me and the other links of 'The Tower' to expect that you would come and ask. I will always be at your service."

"Thank you, I appreciate what you have done for me. I will return home now, Link One," I say tiredly.

"That is quite all right, King William. Have a good trip home," Link One says, and then signs off. I say thank you and I prepare for an immediate departure from Brioche and for a return to Earth.

I call Noor, and I tell her briefly what was discussed, and she did not seem too surprised. She asked me if I was starting to accept the merger now.

I said, "I am. Considering the weirdness of the

circumstances."

"You will be fine, Will. Are you visiting Freedom on your way home to Earth?" Noor asks with concern.

"Not this time, Serena (Noor). I must get back to looking at King George's research. I assure you that I will not be a stranger next time, and I will visit," I reply.

"See you soon, Will," Noor says.

"Absolutely," I reply, and I sign off.

I started to accept the unfathomable destiny that I have, which was planned for me in advance by the mysterious Larip, outside our time.

After departing Brioche, I set course for Earth and four hours later, I arrived home at one a.m. local time.

It was a new experience for me, moving about the White Palace in the early hours of the morning. The night staff were surprised to see me, as I headed towards the Informal Dining Room. I enter the room and I go straight to the autochef, and I order a ham and cheese sandwich, plus an orange juice. Once I have the sandwich and juice, I turn, and I face the lounge area expecting it to be quiet. However, I can see that my wife and sister, along with Charles, Rebecca, Marina, Ann, and Elizabeth, are all sitting quietly. Charles sees me starting to walk over to them, passing the mostly vacant tables in the dining room. The others note the change of expression on his face, and they all turn as one, to face me.

I could see that they wanted an explanation from me, as I arrived at the C-shaped arrangement of sofas. As I sit down, I hold up my hand, indicating that I wanted them to give me a moment before I start to explain my recent actions.

Slowly and carefully, I explain why I needed to go alone. I discuss my meeting with Link One of 'The Tower,' the Sanctuary

Vega Union, as well as the Multiverse Council and the mysterious Larip who exists outside our time. I talk for an hour, in detail, and even though I could see that they were as tired as I was, I could also see that I had their undivided attention. I look at every individual present, and I apologise to them. I sit on the edge of the sofa, and I put my hands to my face after placing my glasses on the coffee table.

Michelle puts her hand on my shoulder gently, and she says softly, "Will, everything is all right now. We were all concerned for you."

"Thank you," I say, in a despondent voice.

"We all watched the rest of that vid, Will. We understand why you were so concerned. It explains a lot about how you have been feeling lately. You do not have to rush back to reviewing King George's research. Just do it when you are ready," Kathryn says.

I did not even notice that as Kathryn spoke to me, she came over and kneeled in front of me. When I remove my hands from my face, I jump slightly with fright and Kathryn places her hands on my knees, saying nothing as she looked into my eyes. At last, I say, "Thanks."

Everyone smiles back at me, and I offer, "I will take a dive in the next minigolf game."

"Only if you want to, sir," Kathryn says, watching my reaction. I nod slowly, and I reach forward to retrieve my glasses from the coffee table, and I resume eating my sandwich.

After I finish the sandwich, I say mysteriously, "The flight home from Brioche was not a dinner flight." Everyone laughs at my joke as we all stand, and we return to our apartments.

It is now two ten a.m., Sunday morning.

Once Michelle and I are in our apartment, we undress and

change for bed in our wardrobes. Later, we lie facing each other on our sides on the bed. I open my mouth to speak, when Michelle places her index finger on my lips, silencing me. "Everything is fine now," she says softly, realising that I must be worried still. She lightly pats my shoulder, and I kiss her in return. Reaching in through the fly of my pyjama bottoms, Michelle starts to stroke my groin, looking into my eyes. I moan with pleasure and Michelle smiles, as she cocks her head slightly, indicating that she wants me to roll onto my back.

Michelle straddles my hips, and she gently lowers herself down onto me. "Thank you, my love," I say with pleasure, as I look into Michelle's eyes.

"You're welcome, sweetheart. I thought that you could do with some stress relief," Michelle says seductively, and we start to move in unison.

Chapter Eight

The Fourth Session

For the next four days, I avoided looking at King George's research on the Dimension War. I did my regular work, and I met with visiting dignitaries. During a working lunch in the Informal Dining Room with my Private Assistants Phoebe Mansfield and Aisha Bacon, I notice Michelle entering the dining room with her assistants and I invite them to join us as the business part of our working lunch had finished.

"When are you going to look at King George's research, sir?" Michelle asks me.

I frown slightly, glance at my assistants, and reply, "After lunch."

"Do you know which data chip?" Michelle asks with interest.

"The last section of the data chip, 'Multiverse Political Structure: The Zlay and the Golden Sceptre'," I reply. Michelle acknowledges me with a nod.

Michelle looks at me closely, after glancing at a wall clock, saying, "I will be able to join you and I know that Kathryn will join us when you look at that data chip. Rebecca will not be joining us, as I know that you are aware that she was on the night shift at the White Palace Medical Service, so she will be catching up on sleep." I nod, confirming that I already knew about Rebecca. I look at my two assistants, who nod in return, and they stand up to leave.

"Was there anything else, Your Majesty?" Assistant Mansfield asks me.

"No, there isn't. Once you both finish doing what you need to do, you can have the rest of the day off. Also, have the notes from my meeting with the Sisss the other day, entered on the deskpad as they haven't yet," I ask.

Aisha and Phoebe look at each other closely, and Aisha says in reply, "It is on your deskpad now, sir. Phoebe did that yesterday afternoon."

I think for a moment, and I recalled that I had seen it on my office deskpad. "Sorry about that. Well done, I had forgotten that I looked at it this morning," I say, shaking my head.

Aisha and Phoebe smile, and they walk away.

Michelle and I leave the Informal Dining Room not long after, and we casually chat as we walk to my Private Office, and enter my study. I was not surprised to see that Kathryn had already arrived.

Kathryn says to me, "I hope that you do not mind that I have already looked at the last part of the vid, the one that you have been talking about. It is not as bad as you think." Kathryn and I stare at each other.

"Okay," I say, trusting my sister's judgement.

I do not know why I was so worried about the final vid as it described in detail the Zlay. We all knew that they are shape-shifting beings, which were once regarded as criminals, or at least not trustworthy. Several Zlay were members of the intergalactic crime fraternity, once known as 'The Shadow'. 'The Shadow' had members from the White Commonwealth which resisted applicants from the Dark Empire. When 'The Shadow' started cooperating with law enforcement throughout the universe, the

Sanctuary Vega Union and the Multiverse Council, the wheels started to fall off the Dark Empire's apple cart. 'Enigma' was still respected by all in 'The Shadow' after becoming a legitimate part of society, not that 'Enigma' was not respected. It had helped that the mysterious leader of 'The Shadow' was me.

The White Commonwealth obtained so much information about the Dark Empire's plans from 'The Shadow,' and soon it became apparent that many beings in 'The Shadow' were not criminals at all, and that included the Zlay. The Zlay are a part of the Larip Alliance, and they are personally connected to the mysterious Larip that created the Golden Sceptre outside of our time. I reflected on why it took so long for the Zlay and Sanctuary to understand their common values.

The Zlay were able to prove to Sanctuary and to Vega that the Kiir could not to be completely trusted, because the Kiir had destroyed the Zlay home universe and had captured the Golden Sceptre from the Larip. Vega rescues the Golden Sceptre from the Kiir, and the Kiir are offered a choice: permanently downgraded in their positions at Vega, or permanent exile.

Now I understood why the Kiir launched the mission to Ancient Egypt. The Kiir wanted the Multiverse to know that they are willing to cooperate with any Sanctuary Vega Union project and prove that they can be trusted; plus, the Kiir knew that they had shown disrespect to Vega and all beings in the universe.

Finally, the vid finishes, and I could tell that everyone was thinking about the implications of the issues raised by the vid, including Multiverse peace. No one spoke for a few minutes, as we all understood that Vega orchestrated the Kiir mission to Earth, for the sole purpose of placing the Golden Sceptre on Earth. Plus, Vega was instrumental in establishing opportunities, and Sanctuary was to follow through and enact the plans for the new universe, and in particular, the creation of the 'Genesis Galaxy' which was the name that the Milky Way was known by the Multiverse, up until humanity became an intergalactic species.

Looking at Kathryn, I say, "I see what you mean." On the surface, it made sense to me, and at the same time, it did not.

Chapter Nine

The Family

Several days later, key members of the family are all seated at a large table in the Informal Dining Room. We had joined together a six-seat table and a four-seat table, so that the ten key members of the royal family did not have to shout across a larger table in the Formal Dining Room.

It was just after breakfast, and we were all chatting casually. Everyone knew that I disliked the Formal Dining Room, and we could not use it anyway due to renovations. As the breakfast regulars left, we prepared ourselves for a more formal meeting, but everyone knew that I liked to keep the relaxed mood going. Artistic members of the family were assisting the decoration of the Formal Dining Room, so that, eventually, the lounge area of the Informal Dining Room extends into the old Formal Dining Room space, which has become a function room.

My quest to get rid of the Formal Dining room is nearly complete.

Recently, I had made a progress report to the Council of Crowns about King George's research. They understood that care needed to be taken with the research, and with the potential to change history, I was told to take as long as I needed.

I was thinking about this when I called for attention, and everyone turns to face me.

"The next data chip in the research sequence is on the

creation of this universe, and of course, the Milky Way. It details the steps taken from the first human spaceflight to the first IGAL low-speed flights to the Andromeda Galaxy and to the Magellanic Clouds. What was known to all, except us, is the name given to our galaxy," I say, watching everyone who acknowledged what is known so far.

"Any ideas?" I ask.

Prince Albert replies, "Sir, are you asking, how do we release the information to the galaxy, and when?" I nod, pleased with the question.

"That is correct, Albert," I answer, looking at everyone.

"We need to release the news in stages, and then explain why," Elizabeth explains.

"That is right, Elizabeth. The mental health issues that would arise consequently, if we didn't release the information carefully," I reply, nodding to Elizabeth.

I look across at Kathryn who nods, and when I look at Michelle, I could see that she was thinking carefully, and then she looks me in the eye, saying, "I know that we are on the right track, but my concern is how Sanctuary, Vega and the Multiverse Council will view the points raised. Particularly, things that could be damaging to them."

"Good point, Queen Michelle," I say. I lightly pat Michelle on the shoulder, and I say, "the Sanctuary Vega Union and the Multiverse Council have assured me that only the Golden Sceptre can decide the outcome."

Kathryn stares at me, and asks uncertainly, "I just want to clarify: you decide?"

"That's right. I decide," I answer, looking at my sister. I add cautiously, "Now you know why, that I have found it hard to accept my own destiny. I was reassured when I went to Brioche the other day that any decision I make will be respected by the Sanctuary Vega Union and the Multiverse Council. I will repeat, that only the Golden Sceptre can decide. I will add that I will accept defeat on the minigolf course."

Everyone laughs at my joke.

"What about Caroline?" Kathryn asks me.

I exchange a glance with Michelle, and Michelle touches my shoulder in reassurance, saying, "Will and I have talked about this, and we both agree that Caroline will understand this as she gets older. Not that I understand what I am about to say fully yet, but Will has told me that we will be able to communicate with him, in a completely normal way after the merger."

Michelle looks at me for confirmation, and I reply, "That's right, my love. Great question, Special K."

Kathryn glares at me, and I remembered that she disliked her childhood nickname. I look at my sister, and I say apologetically, "Sorry, Kathryn." I was worried that Kathryn was upset with me as she stared at me. Suddenly, Kathryn's expression changes, and she starts laughing. Holding up my hands in a conciliatory gesture, I say, "I promise to take a dive in our next minigolf game."

Kathryn smiles as she says, "That will not be necessary, Will. You will lose anyway." Kathryn and I exchange glances, and we nod to each other.

I look at the time on a nearby clock, and I say to everyone, "It is now ten thirty a.m. I want to thank everyone for your attention, and help. If you have nothing on after lunch today, or after breakfast tomorrow, please feel free to join me in my study. It is such a lovely day outside, so let us take the opportunity to change, and join me for a walk in the grounds together. We could take the opportunity to have a barbecue lunch outside, and if we do, standard rules apply, 'no shop talk'. Thank you."

Kathryn looks at the others, replying, "You're welcome, Your Highness." Michelle leans closer to me and kisses me on the cheek, and I give her hand a light squeeze in thanks.

After a pleasant walk through the White Palace grounds, we decided that we will have a light lunch instead in the Informal Dining Room.

Once lunch had finished, Elizabeth, Albert, Edward, George, and Marina had meetings to attend, which left Michelle, Kathryn, Charles, Rebecca, and Ann to join me in my study.

Chapter Ten

The Fifth Session

Looking at the others, I say casually, "After we look at the 'New Universe' data chip, the next data chip in the research sequence is 'Genesis'."

"Isn't Genesis the name that Sanctuary and Vega, have used in the past for the Milky Way?" Rebecca asks.

Turning to Rebecca, I reply, "That's right, Rebecca,"

And then Kathryn asks, "You have been working extremely hard on King George's research lately, have you decided on what you are doing for your annual leave period?"

After glancing at Michelle, I reply, "Michelle and I are going to Vega for two weeks to relax and to refresh at the Summer Palace of Queen Madeira, on the planet Sierra."

Kathryn stares at me, open-mouthed. "You lucky bugger," Kathryn says eventually.

"Is Caroline going with you?" Charles asks.

"Certainly is. This is a family vacation for us, and an educational one for Caroline," I say, nodding to Charles, who had a strange look on his face. I exchange a glance with Michelle, and Kathryn notices.

"What are you *not* saying?" Kathryn asks, with emphasis on *not*.

Smiling, I reply, "As you know, it takes several weeks to get there, but I will be using a trans-universal and trans-dimensional

IGAL ship that is on Earth right now." Kathryn gives me a fixed stare of confusion. I continue to smile, which arouses Kathryn's interest.

"Which ship is it, Will?" Kathryn asks.

"You know the ship. It is the 'Raptor'. The 'Raptor' has these capabilities," I say, as Kathryn frowns in concentration.

I insert the desired data chip into the reader, as I discreetly watched Kathryn's face, and I see her facial expression change when she realises something.

She wags her finger at me saying, "Wait a minute. That was how you got home so quickly after the Virex and Gemini mission. We left at the same time, and you still beat us by at least thirty minutes. That explains why you were coy about the full capabilities of the 'Raptor', and not to mention how you were able to play the practical joke on Michelle and me, with the music of Hall and Oates from the 1980s. 'Private Eyes' if I remember correctly."

Michelle could barely keep a straight face as I reply, "I will not do it again, I promise you." Kathryn scowls at me, and I noticed that she was trying to keep a straight face, and she laughs aloud, breaking the tension.

Smiling, I say, "I am starting the 'New Universe' vid now," as I touch the playback icon on my screenpad, and King George appears on the vidscreen.

King George tells us that the Golden Sceptre knew eons ago that its future home galaxy and its custodian will be in this universe, which is being specifically created to unify the warring universes. Normally, the Multiverse Council never gets involved in the childlike fights, but every now and then, they act. The creation of this new universe is a reminder to all. Behave or else.

None of this was new to me, but it was a revelation to my

companions in my study.

It was the Kiir who put forward the idea to design and construct the 'Wanderer'. The Multiverse Council, as well as the Sanctuary Vega Union, thought that the idea was sensible. The Kiir started the massive project, and fifty thousand years later, the 'Wanderer' is finished, and it is sent off on its quest, from the Kiir enclave in the Gtza universe, as a permanent reminder to all in the Multiverse.

"Peace in our time" was the slogan used to promote the 'Wanderer's' mission.

The power of the Golden Sceptre was understood by all, and even the warring universes feared what it could do, so they relented. The Sti, Xyro, and Gtza ceased all military action, paving the way for the new universe to be created.

On-screen, King George is replaced by Sa-Sisss, the previous incarnation to the Sisss I know. Michelle and Kathryn glance at each other, and then at me.

Sa-Sisss describes how the plans for the creation of the new universe will proceed. The Sti, Xyro and Gtza assist the Multiverse Council to set the detonation sequence of the doom weapons that they created, and initialization of the destruction sequence. Sa-Sisss specifies that this is the moment that the humans call the "Big Bang".

King George re-appears on-screen, and he explains that what Sa-Sisss had talked about was a recording that was submitted to the Permanent Council of Sanctuary, Vega, and the Multiverse Council, not long before their current regeneration. The new universe is monitored closely by the Larip, and King George tells us that the Golden Sceptre has fallen silent, waiting to merge with its permanent custodian. Finally, the Sanctuary Vega Union logo appears on-screen, and the next vid title appears, and the viewscreen asks if I want to proceed to the 'Genesis Galaxy'.

"Pause recording and return to standby," I request, and the viewscreen obediently returns to standby.

For a moment, Charles stares at me strangely, and then he asks in a monotone voice, "What is the Sanctuary Vega Union?" I glance at Kathryn and Michelle, and the looks on their faces conveyed what I was thinking: "something is wrong with Charles."

I answer, "It is the official name of the link between Sanctuary and Vega, and it is used in matters relating to the Multiverse Council and the other universes." I lean forward, and I pick up my coffee cup, containing rapidly cooling coffee, and as I start to finish the coffee, I notice that Kathryn, Charles, and Michelle are exchanging glances. They could tell that I was not saying everything.

Michelle asks me, "Could a threat to this universe exist, but in another one?"

Michelle's question was a great question.

"There are remnants of the Gtza universe, which are bunkered down in several universes. These remnants had never agreed to the creation of this universe, and their command-and-control systems were destroyed when their own universe was destroyed. Zlay security forces currently prevent the Gtza from reorganising. There is no love lost between the Gtza and the Zlay anyway, and a threat to this universe is possible, which cannot be disregarded."

"Do you mean that the Zlay have always been allied to Sanctuary?" Kathryn asks with curiosity.

"That's right. To answer the question that you are thinking about, the Zlay knew that one day, humanity will learn the truth about the Zlay, and that the Zlay knew that we were suspicious of them, and they understood why," I reply.

Michelle and Kathryn stare intently at me, and so did Rebecca, Ann, and Charles.

"I am not at liberty to discuss this," I state.

Rebecca asks kindly, "Can we ask why? I can see that you don't look like you are happy to talk about this, and I know that we want to help you." I look at my cousin, and I know that she understands why I feel torn between my duty and my family. "Sorry, Rebecca. As a member of the Multiverse Council, I am not allowed to discuss this, and I wish that I could tell you all. There are technologies that are so far ahead of ours, and even Sanctuary or Vega, and I can assure you that even accidental revelation of this information will have profound culture shock implications." I look at every single person in my study, and I could see that they understood my dilemma.

I must have looked despondent, so Michelle suggests, "We need to take a break before we view the 'Genesis Galaxy' vid. We can come back to it later."

With a deep sense of relief, I say, "Sounds good. We can adjourn to the Lounge Area, and we can come back after dinner, or we can resume after breakfast tomorrow."

"After dinner is fine, and we can take it easy tomorrow, before we depart for Vega," Michelle replies with a smile, and I give her a kiss on the cheek in thanks.

During dinner, we all chat casually, and I told some lame jokes that I knew that Caroline did not think were funny. Caroline scowls for a moment, and then she resumes eating. Tonight, she was going off to play night minigolf. I look at my daughter, wondering how she will cope as the next custodian of the Golden Sceptre. Caroline must have sensed that I was looking at her; she looks at me and she smiles. It was at this point that I understood that my daughter, Caroline, will cope perfectly well.

Michelle lightly places her hand on top of mine, knowing what was going through my mind. Rebecca and Ann smile in reassurance too. Charles, however, gives me a blank stare, and I realised that his personality has changed. I decided that I needed to talk to my sister about her husband, Charles.

Chapter Eleven

Charles

As I looked at Charles, I sensed that Kathryn is looking at me and I glance at her. Kathryn answers me by a slight nod of the head in the direction of Charles. I understood her subtle message, and I say aloud, "I will be resuming looking at King George's Dimension War research after breakfast tomorrow," and the others agree.

The family start to stand to leave, when I ask, "Queen Michelle, Queen Kathryn, and Princesses Rebecca and Ann. Could you please remain as I would like a private word with you?" Charles makes no attempt to leave, obviously sensing that I was going to talk about him.

"Is there something that you need, Prince Charles, as I do need to talk to Michelle, Kathryn, Rebecca and Ann, regarding a committee that they are on as I am patron? This is a confidential meeting that does not require your input, Prince Charles. However, I may need to talk to you later," I say in a dismissive tone. Charles stands, looking at Kathryn, and then he leaves the Informal Dining Room. I nod subtly to a nearby Royal Guard, to have Charles watched closely.

Once Charles has left the room, I sit down and I ask Kathryn, "What's wrong with Charles now?"

Kathryn replies with a worried look on her face, "Sorry, Will. I do not know, and he will not tell me." I look at Rebecca and

Ann expectantly.

"He could be ill," Rebecca replies.

"His forehead is redder than usual but based on what I have been able to discreetly ask him, I think that he may have CovZlay," Ann says looking at Rebecca.

"Okay, how do we find out?" I ask.

"If you give your Zlay Shape-shifter Detector to Kathryn, it will detect if Charles is a Zlay in disguise or if he has been in contact with a Zlay that has the degenerative condition," Ann says to me. I look at Kathryn, and I can see that she is thinking carefully.

"In the last few months, and, in the last two weeks, Charles has been talking in his sleep, and sometimes he walks around our bedroom at night. I am not getting much sleep, Your Highness. From what I know about CovZlay, humans who get infected by it usually survive and it is rarely fatal, and he needs medical attention from a specialist in human and Zlay conditions," Kathryn says with tears in her eyes.

I knew a lot about CovZlay, a lot more than the others realised, so I say, "I will call Queen Noor and ask her if Charles has been in contact, and then I will ask her if Susan is available to help. Rebecca, can you please make the arrangements for Charles to be treated at Sanctuary Medical? Charles was on a negotiation panel with several Zlay about two years ago. Kathryn, here is the detector. You know what to do. If Charles is infected with CovZlay, time is critical. If Charles is not infected with this condition, we will need to consider suspending him from duty for disciplinary reasons."

I hand Kathryn the detector and I ask her, "Has Charles said anything very strange lately?"

"No, Will," Kathryn answers.

"Time is of the essence. If he has CovZlay, please let me know. If he does not have the nastiest degenerative mental health condition in the universe, I also want to know," I say with concern for my best man and cousin.

We all stand, and finally leave the Informal Dining Room.

Later, Michelle and I were in the Monarch's apartment sitting room. We were both very tired. Kathryn had comcalled me, and confirmed that Charles had CovZlay, and that Rebecca had been in touch with Sanctuary Medical. I had also spoken to Queen Noor, and she told me that Charles had not been in touch with her, and that Susan will arrive on Earth in the next twelve hours. There was nothing that I could do, except wait.

After typing and sending a lengthy message to Sanctuary Medical, I ask Michelle, "Are you sure that you still want to go to Vega?"

"Of course, we all need a decent break, and you definitely need a vacation," Michelle replies.

"It is an important break for us as a family, and I know that you are worried about Kathryn and Charles. I have already spoken to Kathryn while you were in your wardrobe, refreshing yourself, and she said that you would be hesitant. She wants you to know that she knows that you need this vacation to Vega," Michelle adds, looking into my eyes.

We embrace each other, and we kiss.

I feel the soft smooth satin fabric of Michelle's chemise on my chest and I know that Michelle can feel my erection. We kiss passionately and with a free hand, Michelle starts to massage my groin. Michelle looks into my eyes, noting the anticipation and my pain. "Everything will be fine, my love," Michelle says softly. We lay down on the bed, and we continue to kiss.

Several hours later, I wake up and I look at Michelle's face.

She was still asleep, and she has a smile on her face as I look at her. I kiss her forehead lightly, which wakes her up.

"What's up?" Michelle asks sleepily, and she opens her eyes.

"Thanks, sweetheart," I say.

"You're welcome," Michelle replies.

At breakfast in the morning, Michelle asks me, "When are you going to look at the 'Genesis Galaxy' vid on the 'New Universe' data chip?" I had been expecting this question for the last couple of days.

"Not until we return from Vega," I answer, looking over Michelle's shoulder. I see Kathryn, Susan, and a very dazed-looking Charles entering the Informal Dining Room. Susan sees me watching, and she smiles as she walks over to our table.

"Good morning, King William and Queen Michelle," Susan says as Michelle turns in her seat, and she nods.

I reply, "Good Morning, Princess Susan. Thanks for coming," as Michelle finishes chewing a piece of toast.

Michelle has a sip of coffee, and she says, "Hi, Susan." Susan smiles and she focuses her attention on me. "That's okay. How do you feel now, sir?" Susan asks.

"Very well, thanks to you," I reply, motioning that Susan can sit down. Susan nods her head in thanks.

"I hear that you and Michelle are going to Vega, King William. I know that you have been working extremely hard on your uncle's Dimension War research lately. Kathryn told me," Susan explains, as I look at Kathryn, who appears to be physically supporting Charles. Susan sees me looking at Kathryn, and she says, "I have sedated Charles and I have administered the first phase of the CovZlay treatment." I nod gratefully to Susan. "You deserve a break, King William. When do you leave?" Susan asks me.

"Tomorrow, around midday. Caroline's coming too," I reply.

"That's great, King William," Susan says with a smile.

Kathryn smiles tiredly and she says, "We are leaving for Sanctuary now." I stand up and I walk over to my sister, and I give her a hug and a kiss.

Facing Charles, I say, "Everything will be all right, Crown Prince. I know that I have been harsh with you in recent times, and for that, I am sorry." Even in his dazed state, Charles's face registers surprise.

"King William, you have nothing to apologise for. I have embarrassed you a few times lately, and I am sorry that I did not ask for help earlier when you offered it. You were doing your duty as king," Charles says in a monotone voice, and he surprises me by extending his hand and I shake his hand. Rebecca and Ann arrive to assist Kathryn and Susan with Charles, and Rebecca and Ann acknowledge me with a nod and a smile. Finally, they leave the Informal Dining Room as soon as Susan is ready.

Chapter Twelve

Vega

After Kathryn and Charles left, Michelle and I have a quiet day, except that I had a vid audience with Cirek. She told me that someone on board the 'Wanderer' had tried to kill her father, King Gyros. I offer help, which was politely rejected, as I had done more than enough for them lately, but Cirek said that she would contact me if assistance was required. Cirek advised me that trade negotiations between the 'Wanderer', Sanctuary and the Multiverse Council must be put on hold for one month as King Gyros recovers from his injuries.

Later, over dinner, I bring Michelle up to date on the situation on board the 'Wanderer'. Marina and Elizabeth arrive as we finish our meal, and Caroline's live-in babysitter arrives to prepare Caroline for bed. Marina looks at me closely as we enjoy our after-dinner coffees.

Marina asks me, "Cousin William, are you still cautious with the 'Wanderer'?" I look at Michelle as we have discussed this a few times since we encountered the 'Wanderer' for the first time on the 'Swordfish' mission.

There was nobody on the nearby tables, but I say carefully, "Absolutely. For a ship of that size and the residential population on board, there will be beings biding their time. Look how long those Zlay prisoners were able to hide on board." Marina nods, knowing what I was thinking, as we had discussed this very point too.

After a good night's sleep, Michelle, Caroline, and I have breakfast together, and Caroline talks excitedly about the trip to Vega. Michelle and I listen, smiling as our daughter talks, and we glance at each other.

"Don't forget to finish your breakfast, darling," Michelle says.

Caroline gives Michelle a look, and she replies, "Yes, Mummy."

Caroline resumes eating her breakfast, and while Caroline is distracted by her breakfast, I say to Michelle, "Kathryn comcalled me yesterday. Charles is doing very well, and he has finished the second phase of the CovZlay treatment."

Michelle was intrigued, and she asks, "When did they arrive at Sanctuary?"

Looking at a nearby wall clock, I reply, "They are arriving in four hours from now. The Helios doctor who treated me is on the Sanctuary Medical IGAL starship that came for Charles." Michelle nods in understanding.

Caroline says suddenly, "Don't forget your breakfast, Daddy."

I glance at Michelle, who grins, trying not to laugh. "Yes, Crown Princess Caroline," I reply, which causes Michelle to laugh. I give Michelle a fixed stare, and in the end, I start laughing too.

A couple of hours later, after a family game of minigolf, Michelle, Caroline, and I board the 'Raptor' with the things we need on board the ship already. We sit down at our respective stations on the flight deck, and Caroline sits beside Michelle at the co-pilot's control pads as I watch from the command pilot's control pads.

"It looks like you have a new instructor, my love," I say to Michelle. Michelle gives me a fixed glare, so I hold my hands up in surrender. "Sorry, Michelle, I couldn't resist it," I say apologetically. Michelle considers my apology, and she starts to smile.

"Your jokes will never be as good as mine," Michelle says, staring at me.

"Touché," I reply.

"It's time to get going," I say, and Michelle nods.

"Prepare for departure," I announce, and Michelle replies, "Ready."

Touching the External Coms Icon on my control pads, I announce, "The 'Raptor' is ready to start." Once the area is clear of hangar personnel, I say, "'Raptor' Initiate pre-flight and start sequence. Auto coms. Manual Control for departure. Auto control for trans-dimensional IGAL flight, all other systems to Flight Ready status." The 'Raptor' acknowledges my request, and it repeats my instructions for confirmation.

"Confirmed," I reply.

"Trans-dimensional IGAL flight to Vega, 'Raptor'," I request.

"Destination Vega. Request acknowledged," replies the ship.

"King William, we are cleared to depart," the 'Raptor' says.

"Thank you," I reply, and I lift the 'Raptor' off the hangar floor, and I hover two metres above the hangar floor. The hangar ceiling is twenty-five metres above the 'Raptor', and I ease the 'Raptor' slowly forward. The height from the hangar floor to ceiling is fifty metres, and I had plenty of space to use. Out of the corner of my eye, I can see Caroline watching with fascination, and quietly. I turn the 'Raptor' left, and I increased the speed to walking pace as the 'Raptor' moves towards, and then out the hangar exit.

Keeping the 'Raptor' at the same level for thirty seconds, I increase the forward speed to eighty kilometres per hour and I raise the nose of the 'Raptor' slightly, increasing our altitude. Once we are fifteen kilometres from the White Palace, I raise the nose of the 'Raptor' again, this time to a fifty-degree angle and I ease the throttle forward again. I touch the 'Activate Sub-Light system' icon on the control pads. The 'Raptor' rapidly gains altitude quickly, climbing up through the Earth's atmosphere.

Once we arrive in Earth orbit, I glance at my wife and daughter.

"Cool," I heard Caroline say.

"'Raptor' increase speed to warp one and once we are clear of the orbit of Mars, increase speed again to warp five until we clear the outer boundary of the Oort Cloud. When we clear the Oort Cloud, increase speed to warp ten until we clear the Milky Way Galaxy. Once clear of the Milky Way, initiate trans-dimensional IGAL flight to Vega. Switch to Auto Control," I request.

"Request acknowledged, King William," the 'Raptor' replies, after repeating my instructions for confirmation.

One hour after we left the Earth, the 'Raptor' announces, "Initiating trans-dimensional IGAL Flight, flight time to Vega is six hours."

"Thanks 'Raptor'," I reply, as I turn to face Michelle and Caroline. I knew that at high IGAL speed, the flight would take eight weeks. I stand up, yawning, and I stretch out my arms. "Time for a break," I say to Michelle.

Michelle replies, "Sounds good, my love." Michelle and Caroline walk over to me, and Caroline gives me a hug, and I could tell that she was enjoying herself. The three of us leave the flight deck and we go to the Crew Lounge to relax.

After we have a bite to eat, and get a refreshing drink from the autochef, Michelle and I sit on a sofa together, looking out at trans-dimensional space. Not long after, Caroline falls asleep on my nearby recliner chair, and Michelle and I continue to look out the viewport, with our arms around each other's shoulders. We enjoy the moment of peace and quiet together.

After our formal welcome to Vega, two days later, Michelle and I relax at the Summer Palace of Queen Madeira, on the tropical island of Endeavour on the planet, Sierra, which is in a binary star solar system called, Shine Gold. I knew that the two stars are in the same stellar class as the Earth's sun, but just over half of the energy output individually, as the two stars orbit each other. Sierra is in the middle of the habitable zone of the binary solar system, which is the equivalent distance of halfway between the Earth and Mars from the sun. The days are thirty-two hours long, which was strange to me at first; however, I knew that from previous experience, I acclimatised quickly to the four hours extra of daylight, and four hours extra of night-time.

Queen Madeira is human and was born in Vega, and she is Queen Noor's cousin. I have known Madeira for as long as Noor, and like Noor, she went to school on Earth. Her husband, Prince Jethro was born in Vega, and he was educated at Sanctuary and Andromeda. I met Jethro many years ago, when I was in the Galactic Navy, and I knew that he was a close friend of Henry, who was engaged to marry my (King William's) sister.

Jethro and I had many things in common, including our minigolf abilities, which cause our wives some distress. Prince Jethro had assisted my uncle, King George, in the latter years of his Dimension War research. Both royal couples kept talking politics to a minimum, and we enjoy each other's company.

Michelle and I relaxed by the pool attached to our quarters, and our only planned event for the day was lunch with Madeira and Jethro, in the Informal Dining Room of the Queen's Apartments. Michelle was dressed in a light green bandeau bikini, and I was wearing board shorts. Caroline was with Suzi, while the other babysitter, Elvira rested before Caroline's next activity.

Michelle turns her head to face me, and she asks me, "Have you heard any more about Charles from Kathryn?"

"Not yet. The second phase of his CovZlay treatment should be completed by now, and the final phase is due to start soon," I explain, looking at Michelle.

Michelle takes off her sunglasses and she asks with interest, "When is the third phase due to start?"

I look at the screenpad on my lap. "According to the schedule that Kathryn sent me, about two hours ago," I reply.

"Have you spoken to Kathryn yet?"

I look at the comcall unit next to me, and I say, "I will call Kathryn now," and I enter the appropriate codes.

Moments later, I am looking at the very tired looking, and annoyed face of my sister. "What is it?" Kathryn snaps irritably.

Glancing at Michelle, I see the look of surprise. I realised that I did not check the local time on Shentar Two, where Kathryn is staying during Charles's treatment. It is two a.m. Shentar Two Local Time according to my screenpad.

"Sorry for the early morning wake-up call, Kathryn," I say apologetically.

By now, my sister was wide awake, and Kathryn replies, her facial expression softening, "That's okay, Will. I am glad you called."

"How is Charles going?" I ask with concern.

Kathryn notes the look on my face, and she replies, "The Helios doctor who treated you has said that Charles will make a complete recovery. The final phase of the treatment locks in the permanence of his recovery. Charles has responded very well to the CovZlay treatment, better than expected from what the doctor has told me."

"That's great, and I am pleased to hear the news. Could you please pass on Michelle's and my best wishes to him?" I say, glad to hear how well the treatment has gone.

Kathryn looks at me thoughtfully. I thought that I could see tears in her eyes, when she says, "I am sorry that I snapped at you, Will. You did not deserve it."

"That's okay, please don't worry about that," I reply.

Kathryn yawns. "Sorry, I am very tired, Will," Kathryn says, and then she asks, "How is Vega?"

"Very good. It is midmorning, and lunch is in three hours. The suns are shining, and we are being refreshed by a cooling sea breeze, as we laze away the morning by a pool. Caroline is being entertained now. It took her a day to get used to the thirty-two-hour long days."

I sneak a look at Michelle, who is watching me closely. "Charles and I are planning to visit Vega soon," Kathryn says.

"You will love it," I say, not noticing that Michelle had got out of her wicker chair, and she stood looking over my right shoulder.

"Hi, Kathryn," Michelle says, near my right ear.

I must have jumped with fright, as Kathryn smiles, and she answers, "Hi, Michelle."

Michelle apologises to me in a unique way: she kisses me passionately, and Kathryn laughs in response.

Michelle sits on my lap after I place my screenpad on a side table. As Michelle talks to Kathryn, I know that she can feel my erection, and she lightly rubs her hands on my legs. Kathryn notices what is going on as she talks to Michelle. I wink at my sister, and Michelle notices Kathryn's reaction.

"Someone is being naughty here," Michelle says, and Kathryn laughs in reply.

Kathryn says, "I will let you two go now."

I reply, "Thanks, Kathryn."

"Thank you for calling. I needed a boost, and I will let Charles know that you called. There is one thing I need to tell you both," Kathryn said.

Michelle and I exchange glances. "What's that?" I ask with curiosity. I place a hand on Michelle's back, waiting for my sister's reply.

"I am pregnant," Kathryn says smiling happily.

"That's great," Michelle replies.

Then I say, "That's fantastic news, my beautiful sister."

"Thank You, Your Highness," Kathryn answers and she yawns again.

"You need your sleep," I say to Kathryn and then we sign off.

Michelle stands up and she looks at my lap. She pretends not to notice my groin and she smiles seductively as I stand up to embrace her. We walk over to the pool, and down the steps into the water. Sitting on a ledge, we have water up to our chests and Michelle and I kiss as she unbuttons the fly of my boardshorts. Michelle reaches inside the fly, and she starts to massage my groin, looking deeply into my eyes.

Over the next ten days, Michelle and I completely relax and unwind. I felt truly refreshed and I knew that Michelle felt the same way. Kathryn keeps us up to date with how Charles is going, and I knew that they were returning to Earth tomorrow, a day and a half before Michelle and I are due to leave Vega. In the last comcall, Kathryn and Charles had only just left Sanctuary, and I could see how much better Charles looked. I was pleased that Charles had recovered completely.

The day before we are due to return to Earth, Michelle and I have a formal lunch with our hosts, Queen Madeira and Prince Jethro. Michelle and I had only two minor engagements during our two weeks at Vega.

Meanwhile, White Palace and Sanctuary Vega Union technicians make sure that the 'Raptor' is ready to depart Sierra, and the Shine Gold Solar System. As always, Sanctuary Vega Union and Royal Security prepare to accompany us on our flight home to the Milky Way.

Chapter Thirteen

The Genesis Galaxy

After a textbook departure from Sierra, we travel at warp ten to the transition point for the trans-dimensional IGAL flight home.

Six hours later, we transition back to IGAL flight on approach to the Milky Way and then we transition further, back to warp flight. One hour later, we arrive on Earth.

When the 'Raptor's' boarding ramp lowers, Michelle, Caroline, and I walk down the ramp. "Welcome home, King William, Queen Michelle and Crown Princess Caroline," Kathryn says with a smile. We hug briefly and I turn my attention to Charles. I ask him how he is feeling, and he tells me that he is back to normal.

"I am having counselling sessions with Princess Susan," Charles says in a tone meant to reassure me. I pat him on the back, and I give Kathryn a kiss, and we leave the White Palace Hangar to return to the Royal Apartments to drop off our hand luggage, and then we continue to the Informal Dining Room for some light refreshments.

It was just after lunch, and Kathryn, Charles, Michelle, and I were enjoying a chicken sandwich and we talk casually. Rebecca, Ann, Elizabeth, and Marina had joined us, and Albert, George and Edward arrived soon after. The C-shaped arrangements of sofas that we chose in the Lounge Area leaves me no room to sit, so I sit on a recliner chair that is between two of the sofas. Eventually, I was asked the two questions that I was expecting: How was Vega? And when was I returning to King George's Dimension War research.

Michelle and I glance at each other briefly, and Michelle talks about what we did at Vega. I say that I considered when I would resume reviewing King George's Dimension War research, and that I will be focusing on the 'New Universe' data chip, and, especially, the 'Genesis Galaxy' vid. No one says anything for a moment. Personally, I was dreading looking at the research, but I knew that I must, and I had to admit that I was curious.

I decided to resume the research review immediately, so I ask if anyone wants to join me in my study. Charles and Kathryn offer to join me straight away as they were planning to return to Centauri in a few weeks' time. The Council of Crowns offered to continue to look after the day-to-day affairs of the White Commonwealth, and they said that they were looking forward to my report. Rebecca, Marina, Ann, and Elizabeth say that they will join me as well, as they have a few days break, and they wanted to assist my quest.

My personal commlink chimes, and I answer, "What is it?"

"Sir, sorry for the late notice; the Prime Minister has arrived for an audience and so has Admiral M for a separate audience. This item was not taken out of your diary as the Council of Crowns. The Council apologised that they didn't realise that you wanted these meetings to be deferred for twenty-four hours.

"Okay. Could you please tell the Prime Minister that I will be there in about five minutes and let Admiral M know that I will be with him as soon as possible after my audience with the PM?" I say, half expecting this to occur.

"All done, Your Highness," Assistant Bacon replies, and

Assistant Bacon signs off.

I look at the others and say, "Sorry, I can't resume the research review today. It will have to be tomorrow after breakfast."

Everyone looks at each other, and then finally at me.

Kathryn says, "No problem. If we don't see you tonight for dinner, we will see you in your Private Study after breakfast."

I stand, and I indicate that no one needs to stand.

Turning to Michelle, I say, "See you later, Sunshine." Michelle nods, smiling and I walk away from the Lounge Area, and I go directly to my office suite.

At four thirty p.m., I leave my office suite as I have finished my regal obligations for the day, and I return to my apartment. When I enter my sitting room, I see that Michelle is typing on her screenpad, she looks up smiling at me. I couldn't see or hear Caroline.

"Where is Caroline?" I ask.

"Caroline is with Elvira. She is playing minigolf with school friends," Michelle replies.

Michelle gives me a look of concern as she seems to notice that there is something wrong, so she asks me what's wrong. Normally I do not tell her what has been discussed in audiences that she doesn't attend.

Thinking carefully, I say, "I feel like a walk outside, in the grounds." Michelle nods, knowing that I wanted to say something particularly important.

I change into track pants, and I take off my polo shirt that I wore on the flight home. Michelle changes into a T-shirt and training leggings. Once we are both ready, we leave the apartments, and we start walking. Once we arrive at the outdoor picnic tables, I sit down, and I tell Michelle what the Prime

Minister and Admiral M had said.

When I finish talking, Michelle says, "We need to be careful then, that is, if it is true. Do we tell Kathryn and the others?"

"We will, but not immediately, the threat is being monitored by the Zlay, 'The Tower' and the Sanctuary Vega Union. I don't like to say this but please do not tell them. I don't want them worried," I say.

Michelle gives me a concerned look, knowing that we both knew as much as each other. "Has 'The Shadow' provided any information?" Michelle asks.

"Not yet. I have been in touch with Des, who runs the 'Abyss.' He has said that he has seen her, and if true, a renewed danger to galactic harmony could emerge," I say quietly as palace staff walked past the tables, nodding to me.

"What will you tell the Council?" Michelle asks.

"I will tell them that there will be no change to anything we do," I reply.

"Do you think that it is true?" Michelle asks me anxiously.

"I would be surprised if it is not. The Royal Security Service, Royal Guard, the Sanctuary Vega Union, and Sanctuary have been advised. There will be no visible change to procedures anywhere, just yet. She is hiding in plain sight, not realising that she has been spotted. She cannot move anywhere without us knowing where she is. Also, she may think that the procedures that she has undergone have fixed her problems. Certain items used in her original treatment are still highly classified. These things cannot be detected," I explain.

"I feel like an early dinner," I say to Michelle as we stand up, and start walking back to the Royal Apartments entrance.

"How about we watch the vidscreen movie, *Apollo 13* after dinner?" Michelle asks, as we walk. I had forgotten that I wanted to watch this movie.

"Okay, great idea," I say, and then I add quietly, speaking next to Michelle's left ear, "We can't take any chances with Mara this time. When we do catch her, I know what I have to do." Michelle stares at me as I stand facing her.

"I know that you don't want to do this, but you know that is your duty," Michelle says looking closely at me.

I look at the doors to the Royal Apartments, and the Royal Guard at the doorway was wondering why I stopped.

"Mum's the word," I say to Michelle, and she repeats it back to me and then we go inside.

After breakfast the next morning, Kathryn, Charles, Michelle, Rebecca, Marina, Ann, and Elizabeth join me in my Private Office Study, and we all sit facing the viewscreen. I insert the data chip into the reader, and the 'Genesis Galaxy' vid starts to play. There was a brief introduction, and I wondered why the focus on the Milky Way Galaxy itself. I started to get the strange feeling that we are going to see how Earth's solar system was created, and then I remembered that that is on the next vid on the data chip. Looking at Michelle, I can see that she is thinking the same way as me, and that includes the thing that I am not talking about just yet: Mara's reappearance.

Kathryn and Charles glance at me, and I knew that they were thinking about the Golden Sceptre as they don't know about the other issue yet. I was dreading telling them. So, I shrug my shoulders in response. Kathryn was looking at me closely, and I knew that she knew that it wasn't the Golden Sceptre which was on my mind.

Looking at the viewscreen, we see a deskpad simulation of the formation of the Earth's solar system, and then, actual footage of the various stages of the solar system's formation. I had forgotten that this is the brief overview of what is in the next vid, and the classified data chips that the others did not know about yet. I couldn't help thinking what twenty-first century Astrophysicists, Physicists, Astronomers, and other scientists would think of this material.

A Helios appears on the screen and introduces their name, Zaa. I let out an involuntary gasp, as I had only heard about this legendary figure in Helios Society and the Multiverse.

"Are you all right?" Michelle asks with concern.

"That is Raa and Hgh's ancestor. The Helios equivalent of Albert Einstein," I reply, watching the screen. I apologise for startling the others as the others watch in fascination.

"Makes sense," Kathryn says, giving me that look again.

Zaa confirms the uniqueness of the Earth in the Multiverse.

Zaa says, "The Golden Sceptre of Vega has indicated that this solar system will be its home. The third planet will become known as the Earth. The final stage of this vid is about the Earth itself."

"Pause vid," I request, and the image on the vidscreen freezes.

I look slowly at every single person in my study.

"Where are George, Albert and Edward?" I ask.

Rebecca replies, "They have no engagements at the moment, as they are due to leave the solar system for their home systems tomorrow."

"Can you please tell them to come here immediately, as I have a serious matter to discuss with you all?" I ask anxiously.

Kathryn asks, "What's wrong?"

"I have to wait until the guys get here," I say, in a tone indicating that I was genuinely concerned about something. Michelle looks at me sympathetically, knowing what I was about to say.

Six minutes later the three princes enter my study, and I knew that the Royal Guard in the room knew what I was about to talk about.

Without fanfare, I say, "Sorry to disrupt the routine today, but I have something of extreme importance to discuss." Everyone in the crowded room nod encouragingly. "You all know about the audiences that I had separately yesterday, with Admiral M and the Prime Minister. It was about the same subject. What I am about to tell you has a security level of Royal Quadruple Alpha," I say, pausing to take a drink. Everyone knew that this high-security level is for me as Monarch normally. Michelle was nodding encouragingly.

"All of you are aware of Des, the owner of a bar called the 'Abyss' on a planet that I will call X. Its actual name and location can only be known to me personally. A mysterious woman in her late fifties entered the bar recently and has become a regular customer. She is also a provider of certain services." Everyone gives me a blank look, not understanding what I was talking about.

"You will understand, when I finish talking," I say.

Kathryn gives me the strange look that she has given me a few times lately, and she knows that I am close to saying something. "Who is the person that Des has seen?" Kathryn asks. I nod gratefully to my sister, as she seemed to grasp the situation better than anyone else, except for Michelle, who knew already.

"Mara is alive," I say simply.

"What?" Kathryn asks.

"Apparently a mysterious ship was able to teleport the Dark Emperor from her prison asteroid, less than a second before the chunk of the Kiir freighter hit the asteroid," I say.

"The Sanctuary Vega Union, 'The Tower', the Multiverse Council, and the Council of Crowns have been informed by A1 Shentar as the Shentar Leadership are responsible for the safety of the Golden Sceptre," I explain.

"Good Lord, do we know anything else, cousin?" Marina asks with a look of shock on her face.

"Not yet, the Zlay Security Force, Sanctuary Security, 'The Tower', and Multiverse Security have our friend contained, and she cannot leave the planet concerned as 'The Shadow' have control of all starship movements in the system. Mara has had restorative surgery that has restored just about everything, except for the secret items implanted in her body and skull that cannot be detected," I say, feeling relieved.

"Not a word to anyone about this," I order everyone.

"Yes, Your Majesty," everyone in the room says as one.

"When we do move on her, she will wonder what has hit her. She will have the same surgery again, and I know that she loves symbolism. The Council of Crowns agrees with the Sanctuary Vega Union decision made, that authorises her execution, and they have decided only the Golden Sceptre can decide on the method of execution, or if she is allowed to live. There is a total media blackout on this matter, and on the surface no procedures of ours are being changed, which might be taken as a warning to Mara. I do not like the fact that she has to be executed, but I have decided to do this personally, when the time is right. Any questions?" I ask. There were no questions; they all agreed anyway.

"In order to keep this quiet, we also need to act as if nothing is unusual. It's time for lunch. We can play minigolf afterwards and tomorrow, we can watch the 'Earth' vid."

"Sounds great, Will," Kathryn says smiling.

Chapter Fourteen

Venus

After lunch, we all make our way to the minigolf course for a thrilling, action-packed game. In the final round, Michelle and I beat Kathryn and Charles. Kathryn glared at me, annoyed that I won, but I knew that it was in jest. There was a strange feeling of tension the entire time we were at the minigolf course, and I knew that it had nothing to do with Michelle and I winning.

Michelle says to me quietly as we return to the Royal Apartments, "Maybe it wasn't a clever idea, telling them about Mara."

"It had to be done. If I had said nothing, and if Mara suddenly reappeared standing in the middle of Swanston Street in Melbourne, outside Flinders Street Station, then there would have been a mass panic," I reply in an agitated tone.

By this time we had entered our apartment, and Michelle snarls, "Don't be sarcastic."

I stare at Michelle for a moment, as we stand in our sitting room. I was grateful that Caroline was at school because Michelle and I rarely argued. We have always been of the same mind on many occasions, and when we didn't agree, we normally worked out a compromise.

Michelle sits down on a sofa, and she seems surprised that I wasn't sitting down with her. I simply turned around, and I walked straight out before she could say something. I go down the corridor, taking a travelator as if I were in a hurry. Problem was, I wasn't in a hurry. I get off the travelator, and I walk to the access lifts to the White Palace Hangar. I had already switched my personal portable comcall unit to 'Do not Disturb'.

I wasn't upset with Michelle, and I was thinking what to say to her. Mara's re-emergence could destabilise the White Commonwealth, and I was worried that if Mara had found a way to counter the Golden Sceptre, then she would use it. The problem with that is, Mara is hiding in plain sight, which tells me that she is on a fishing expedition.

With that assumption in mind, I ride the lift to the White Palace Main Hangar floor. I seemed to surprise the afternoon shift as I walked purposefully through the hangar towards the 'Raptor'. The Chief Engineer greets me as normal, and I ask her if the 'Raptor' is ready for flight. She consults her screenpad and her assistant checks a deskpad nearby.

"Yes, Your Highness. The 'Raptor' is ready for departure," the Chief Engineer says nodding to me.

"Thanks for that," I reply. The Chief Engineer nods and then turns away to speak to a technician.

I walk to the 'Raptor' and I use the boarding ramp to enter the ship, and the ramp retracts automatically as I walk to the flight deck.

"Good afternoon, 'Raptor'. Could you please send an audio message from me to Queens Michelle and Kathryn, Crown Prince Charles, and Princesses Rebecca and Marina, asking them to come here? Tell them once they arrive, I will lower the boarding ramp for them," I ask.

"Certainly, sir," the 'Raptor' replies.

A couple of seconds later, the 'Raptor' announces, "Queens Michelle and Kathryn, Crown Prince Charles and Princesses

Rebecca and Marina are on their way, King William."

"Did they sound concerned?" I ask.

"They did, but they are on their way," the 'Raptor' replies.

Within about ten minutes, all five members of the royal family are outside the 'Raptor'. I lower the boarding ramp and they all walk up the ramp and into the ship. Once they were safely aboard, I retract the ramp and I announce over the internal intercom system, "Sorry about the mystery, prepare for departure, please remain in the Crew Lounge until I say so."

To the 'Raptor' I say, "Auto Pre-Flight and Pre-start Sequence and Auto Coms. Auto Departure and Auto Control for flight to Venus and landing on Venus." The 'Raptor' repeats my instructions to me. 'Raptor', like the 'Swordfish', can operate in any environment or existence, and the 'Raptor' has been on planets far more hellish than Venus before.

Once we are out in space, heading for Venus, I remember my passengers.

"Could everyone please come up to the flight deck and take up your usual positions, please?" I say.

Moments later, everyone arrives on the flight deck and sit at their respective stations.

Firstly, I face Michelle, seated at the Science station. "Michelle, you were right, and I apologise for walking out on you earlier. I was extremely rude," I say apologetically.

Michelle gives me a smile in reply, and says, "Don't worry about it, Will. It was a judgement call that you had to make. I realised that after you left the apartment. I know that you were not being sarcastic, and I am sorry that I made that remark," Michelle says looking closely at me.

I smiled, and I said, "Thanks, Michelle." Michelle returns the smile.

Slowly, I explain why we are in space approaching Venus.

"Approaching Venus orbit, sir," the 'Raptor' announces.

"Thanks 'Raptor'," I reply. I look around the flight deck, looking at intrigued faces. I laugh at the sight, and I say to 'Raptor', "Continue with auto approach and landing at set coordinates," I request.

"Yes, sir," the 'Raptor' answers.

Out of the corner of my eye, as I monitored our descent into the Venusian atmosphere from my control pads, I could see the open mouth stares of the others.

Thirty seconds later, the 'Raptor' announces, "King William. We are now hovering at one hundred and fifty metres above the landing coordinates. The base weather station reports that the wind is coming from the west, speed eighty-five knots. Current air temperature is four hundred and ninety-eight degrees centigrade, and the Inferno Base transponder has responded to my ping; the hangar airlock is ready to receive us," the 'Raptor' says.

"Thanks, 'Raptor'. Initiate auto vertical descent," I say.

Looking out the flight deck viewport, we could see how uninviting it looked outside the 'Raptor'. It was very dull, with dark heavy clouds, and I could see lightning a couple of kilometres away. Inferno Base is inside a wide valley, where at one time liquid water had flowed millions of years ago and there was a canyon several kilometres to the west. The light level looks like early evening on Earth, even though local time was midday, and the sun is almost directly overhead.

With the lightest touch, the 'Raptor' lands on a platform that starts to descend. I switch a viewscreen to show the view above us, and we see the vertical shaft darken as the first set of hangar doors close. A second and a third set closes and then the platform moves forward into a massive, well-lit hangar. The landing platform turns the 'Raptor' around, to face the way it entered the base hangar. We see the final door slide closed.

"Shutdown complete," the 'Raptor' says.

"Activate standby mode," I request.

"Standby mode is now active," the 'Raptor' says.

I stand and face the others who couldn't help staring out the viewports, as they could see people and robots moving about.

"Welcome to Inferno Base. The hangar itself has an Earth standard atmosphere, so we do not need to use a boarding tube to exit the ship. We are protected from the hostile environment on the surface by four sets of hangar doors and environment containment fields at every set of doors," I say as the others walk over to me.

"Why are we here?" Charles asks.

"I am showing this facility to you because this base was built for my father, to protect me as the Golden Sceptre. The Sanctuary Vega Union and the Multiverse Council constructed this facility for him to facilitate his request. Let's go to the Control Room level and I will take you to the office suite so we can continue our discussion about Mara. I am intending to stay here for about one hour, before we depart for Earth. Follow me, please," I say, as we exit the flight deck and leave the 'Raptor' via the boarding ramp.

Kathryn, Michelle, Charles, Rebecca, Marina, Ann, and Elizabeth follow me to the office suite. Once we enter the office suite, we go straight to the office I use when I am at Inferno Base. Indicating the autochef, I say, "Feel free to get something to eat or drink."

I sit down on a sofa, and the others sit on sofas that form a square shape.

"I cannot stress the importance of being careful, that is, if the report is true about the former Dark Emperor. The latest report that I have received from Des, and 'The Shadow' confirms that Mara has settled down, and is actually working as a prostitute," I explain.

"Why on Planet X?" Rebecca asks.

- "Planet X is in a solar system that is in the Large Magellanic Cloud, so, close enough to the Milky Way so that she does not have to travel too far. We have found out that she was rescued by an associate that slipped through the net when the Dark Empire fell. I was informed that she didn't enjoy her time in Stanton's Void where she was hiding," I explain.

Michelle looks closely at me. "What's the plan, Will?" she asks.

"Basically, what I mentioned in my study. Mara is under total surveillance, and she cannot move if she wanted to. When we are ready, we will purposefully let her know that she is being watched, and we will be in control of where she goes. Eventually, the Scrapper and Enigma will contact her to assist her. She will have the same medical treatment again, but we will shut down her ability to speak after I have a friendly chat with her," I say.

Kathryn asks, "You said something about Mara and symbolism?"

"That's right. I am going to make her feel the same way our father felt when he was about to die. Seriously, I wish that I didn't have to be the last face that she sees before her death. I wish that I didn't have to do the task required, but I must. The danger she poses to the entire universe is massive. Putting her inside another prison asteroid will mean that she could be rescued again. As the Golden Sceptre in human form, I know that she can never win. I just want her to think that she can win. It is a simple game of cat and mouse," I explain.

I could sense the consensus of everyone in the room. They knew my personal feelings on the subject, and the concerns that I had about my merger with the Golden Sceptre after my death, and, currently, my more serious concern is about the former Dark Emperor.

"Any questions?" I ask. There were no questions.

"Melbourne time is now four p.m.," I say looking at my screenpad.

"Take the chance to have another drink, or quickly refresh now, before we depart from Venus in about thirty minutes from now. I will give you a very quick guided tour of Inferno Base as we head for the hangar level," I say casually.

Each member of the party was amazed at the sights of the underground base.

The ground shook slightly.

"That was a typical Venusquake. Very slight. The good thing is that this base has a similar design to a base that is on a geologically continually active world. The base uses gravimetric control systems that can counter the effects of anything up to and well past a singularity forming, right here," I say, pointing at the ground.

We arrive back at the 'Raptor' and board the ship to prepare for departure.

"Auto Coms. Auto Pre-Flight and Pre-Start sequence. Initiate Base Exit procedure, 'Raptor'. Auto start sequence once we get to the surface. Manual Control departure from the landing pad. In-flight control auto at my command. Initiate Approach and Landing on Earth. Auto Shutdown after landing," I request.

Once we arrive at the surface, I pull back slightly and the

'Raptor' hovers just above the landing pad. I activate the sublight systems and the 'Raptor' starts moving forward, gaining speed. Pulling back again, I apply maximum thrust and we start climbing through the Venusian atmosphere quickly. Once we are in space, climbing towards orbit, I say, "Auto Control. Sub-warp flight to Earth. Auto Control for approach and landing on Earth."

Twenty-five minutes later, we are descending through the Earth's atmosphere, and another eight minutes later, we have landed inside the White Palace Hangar.

As we leave the 'Raptor' I say, "Thanks for your assistance, guys. The rest of the afternoon is yours. See you at dinner tonight if you have no engagements. I will be looking at King George's Dimension War research tomorrow after breakfast, and, in particular, the 'Earth' vid. Feel free to join me if you can, and thanks again for your support."

"You're welcome, Your Majesty," Kathryn says to me as we walk away from the ship.

Chapter Fifteen

Earth

Michelle and I spend the rest of the afternoon in the sitting room of our apartment. We were both working on our own screenpad, sitting at either end of the casual dining table. I could have gone to my office to catch up on a dreaded amount of paperwork, but I chose to spend my time working with my wife catching up on her paperwork.

"Damn it!" I heard Michelle exclaim a couple of times.

I look up, and I ask interestedly, "What's wrong, Michelle?" She looks at me, shrugging her shoulders and nodding her head in the direction of her screenpad.

"This screenpad is playing up. I have just completed my weekly report to the Council of Crowns, and when I try sending it to the duty officer for the Council, it doesn't go through," Michelle says.

"I have finished my boxes; can I help you, my love?" I offer.

Michelle replies, "If you could, that would be great."

I change seats to a chair on the side of the table and Michelle sits next to me.

Visually, I check the screenpad for any damage. Nothing appeared to be wrong.

I ask Michelle if she minds if I activate the reset function.

Michelle says, "That's okay. When I tried it, the screen went blank."

Nodding, I use the reset function.

The screenpad resets and I cross my fingers.

I could see that Michelle's report was still there, and I beam a copy of the report to my screenpad, and I hear the screenpad beep as normal.

Michelle watches with fascination as I check Michelle's document on my screenpad. There was nothing wrong with the document at all, so I send it to the duty officer of the Council of Crowns. The duty officer replies that the document has been received.

I look at Michelle, and I say to her casually, "I will get you a new screenpad."

I pick up my personal comcall unit from the table in front of me, and I call my duty assistant, "Aisha, can you please bring me a new screenpad from my stock, and have it set up with my profile, but use Queen Michelle's name? Also, can you please let the Queen's assistant know that her profile needs to be checked before you bring the screenpad to my apartment?"

"Certainly, King William. I will do that now. I will be there in about ten minutes, is that okay?" Aisha asks.

"That's fine, Aisha," I answer.

Eight minutes later, Aisha is guided into my sitting room, and she hands the new screenpad to me. I was impressed how quickly Aisha was able to respond. "Thanks, Aisha. What was the problem with Michelle's profile?" I ask.

"Admin Technology Services had forgotten to inform the Queen that they were running a system test," Aisha says looking from me to Michelle.

Looking at Michelle, I say to Aisha, "Aisha, please remind Admin Technology Services that they need to communicate with the staff and household members before these checks are carried out. You can tell them that I personally request that they must run their tests on the simulator system first."

"Yes, Your Highness," Aisha says smiling, knowing that Admin Technology Services frustrate the staff and household alike, and Aisha nods at Michelle and I before leaving the sitting room.

I hand the new screenpad to Michelle saying, "I have sent off the document that you were trying to send to the duty officer for the Council of Crowns. All done."

Michelle looks at her new screenpad nodding in approval and she gives me a kiss. "Thank you, my love," Michelle says, placing her screenpad on the table.

We both hear our daughter arriving with Suzi, so we turn our seats around to watch our daughter enter the sitting room.

Caroline expertly sidesteps Suzi and her security escort, and then runs over to Michelle and me. Caroline hugs and kisses Michelle, and then she turns to me, walks an extra step, and she hugs me too. She gives me a kiss on the cheek saying, "Hi, Daddy." I look over to a smiling Suzi who nods, and to Caroline's escort who smiles and nods as well.

I nod gratefully, saying to Caroline, "Hi, Caroline. Have you been good?"

"Yes, Father," Caroline says confidently.

"It's time for your dinner, Caroline," Suzi says, looking at the nearby wall clock.

"Okay, Suzi," Caroline replies.

"Suzi, how is your father now?" I ask, knowing that he had recently had surgery.

"Very well, sir. He has recovered, and he is now resting at home. I will let him know that you asked how he is," Suzi says looking at me.

"I hope to catch up with him soon. I may need his advice on something," I say thinking carefully.

Suzi smiles broadly, and she replies, "I am sure that he would be happy to help you, sir. My father has told me about some of the things that you have done together over the years," Suzi says.

Returning Suzi's smile, I reply, "It was an honour to serve with him. As I said before, it would not be a difficult task. I can arrange for an audience here, or I can visit him. Please let me know what he prefers."

"I will do that, sir," Suzi says, as she holds Caroline's hand and they walk out of the apartment.

After dinner, Michelle and I returned to our apartment as we were going to watch a vidscreen movie and refresh for bed, and I could tell that there was something on Michelle's mind.

"Will, what are you going to ask Suzi's father?" Michelle asks as we sit down on our own sofa.

Looking at Michelle, I reply, "He may have ideas about Mara."

"What sort, if you don't mind me asking?" Michelle asks with interest.

I tell Michelle about Suzi's father, Commander Adrian and how he was my intelligent weapons systems officer on the 'Australis', and his work with me in 'The Shadow'.

Michelle's jaw drops. "So, he was the one that developed the EMP weapon that you used to disable the Dark Emperor's prison asteroid," Michelle asks when she regains her composure.

"Bingo. He still has the highest-level Galactic Navy security clearance, and there is the small matter that he is Queen Allison of Spica's son," I say. Michelle grins at me which surprises me a little.

"I already knew that from my father," she says.

"Touché," I reply, smiling at Michelle.

"That's enough shop talk," Michelle says, wagging her right finger at me.

"Are we going to watch the movie?" Michelle asks, knowing that I loved comedy films.

"Okay. Boss," I say, stifling a laugh.

After breakfast the next morning, I had a Council of Crowns meeting where I updated the Council on the latest information that we had regarding Mara, and my progress on King George's Dimension War research. I advised them that I am resuming the research after the meeting. I also stress the appearance of normality that we need to maintain until Mara is captured, and the media blackout that is needed.

The Council assures me that they support the decision that I have made.

Returning to my study, I was not surprised to see Kathryn and Charles, Michelle, Rebecca, Marina, Ann, and Elizabeth already waiting.

I place the data chip containing the overview of the Earth's evolution, into the reader.

"Thanks for joining me once again," I say, touching the play icon.

We see highlights of the Earth's evolution, including when humans first emerged on Earth. Everyone was fascinated, including me. I wondered what the early humans that we were seeing on the 4D viewscreen would think if they knew that they were being observed. It reminded me of a vidscreen movie that I saw years ago, called *The Truman Show*, about a baby being brought up by a corporation, documenting every moment of the newborn baby's life to adulthood, and broadcasting every moment live on television.

Finally, the event that I was expecting to see, appears on-screen.

It was the Kiir mission to Earth, when the Kiir present the Golden Sceptre to Pharaoh Khasekhemwy of Egypt during the Second Dynasty. We see the complete mission vid. Zaa describes that this event was the biggest event in Multiverse history. In other words, the Golden Sceptre was about to guide humanity towards its destiny. The others stare at me in sympathy, finally understanding why I have been so anxious about my destiny.

The playback finishes, and everyone looks at each other. "Any questions?" I ask, and there were none, only looks of sympathy.

Chapter Sixteen

In Reflection

Several days later, I sit with Kathryn, Michelle, Charles, Rebecca, Ann, Elizabeth, and Edward in the Lounge Area of the Informal Dining Room. I say to them that it was still too soon to draw conclusions about King George's Dimension War research, as the ramifications of culture shock are great, even with the issue of Mara's re-appearance. We all knew that care is needed when we release the findings of the research.

Members of the family contributed their ideas during the discussion. I was grateful for Charles's insight, now that he has fully recovered from CovZlay. Kathryn and Charles had been asking many questions about Vega, as they are looking forward to their vacation. Kathryn was looking forward to becoming a mother too.

It was at this point that the White Commonwealth was shaken to the core.

The day after a regular Council of Crowns meeting, Michelle, Caroline, and I were playing minigolf, when my personal comcall unit chimes unexpectedly.

"What is it?" I ask, and my personal assistant replies in a strained voice.

"Sir, I have just been informed that King James has just died," Assistant Aisha says. Michelle notes the strange look on my face and seems to get the gist of the call.

I was shocked. King James was ninety-nine years old, and he was in perfect health, and I knew that he was physically fit too.

"How did it happen?" I ask.

"His doctor has told me that he complained of a migraine headache when he woke this morning, and the doctor checked him with a medi-scanner. It detected a serious brain aneurysm that was previously unknown, and it was worsening by the second. Sadly, King James died before he could be taken to the White Palace Medical Service," Aisha says with a sniff.

I say to Aisha in a kind voice, "Please ask Phoebe to assist you. Thanks for letting me know and I appreciate your service. Can you please get Queen Kathryn, Crown Prince Charles, Princesses Rebecca and Marina to meet Michelle and I in my apartment's sitting room in thirty minutes? And please do not mention the reason."

"Yes, sir and thank you. Phoebe is already here," Aisha says, and she signs off.

We left the minigolf course immediately, and we board our surface transport which takes us back to the Royal Apartments. As this happens, I explain what has happened to Michelle, and she was as shocked as I was.

After sitting down in our sitting room, Elvira comes to look after Caroline. I made sure that both babysitters knew what had happened by sending them an e-message during the journey from the minigolf course.

Kathryn, Charles, Rebecca, and Marina arrive, and they wait patiently for me to indicate that it is okay for them to sit down. They sit down exchanging looks, and they could tell that the news was going to be bad.

I get straight to the point, and I tell them what happened, and

Kathryn looks at Charles, and she offers to defer their vacation to Vega. My concern was for them, as Charles had only just recovered and that Kathryn was pregnant, and I tell them that they can still go.

Kathryn looks at me sympathetically, knowing how close I was to King James, and she says, "We can wait, so we can all go together, and I know that you and Michelle are due to go back to Vega in three weeks for the meeting with Noor, Madeira, the Zlay High Councillor and the Shentar Leadership. We will have plenty of time to relax then," Kathryn says kindly.

I nod gratefully to my sister and tears start to well up in my eyes. Michelle puts her arm around me, and she says to comfort me, "It's okay to grieve, Will. You and Kathryn both loved your uncle."

Looking at Kathryn, I can see the tears in her eyes, and I start to stand. Michelle knows that I want to comfort my sister. I embrace Michelle and I give her a kiss in gratitude, and I turn to Kathryn. I embrace my sister who has started to cry, saying nothing.

Kathryn says softly in my ear, "Thanks, Will," and she stops crying.

The thing that comforts me the most is knowing that the former Dark Emperor will soon be facing her own destiny.

The End

Other book in the Sanctuary Series
Published by Olympia Publishers

Other books in the Sanctuary Series:

Prelude to Sanctuary (Book One) by Gavin Catt
Sanctuary (Book Two) by Gavin Catt
Project Genesis (Book Three) by Gavin Catt

Coming Soon in the Sanctuary Series:
Sanctuary: Destiny (Book Four) by Gavin Catt
Sanctuary: Destiny (Book Five) by Gavin Catt